A STONE WATERMELON

A Stone Watermelon

Lois Braun

Turnstone Press

Published with the assistance of the Manitoba Arts
Council and the Canada Council.

Turnstone Press
607-99 King Street
Winnipeg, Manitoba
Canada R3B 1H7

This book was typeset by Communigraphics and
printed by Hignell Printing Limited for Turnstone
Press.

Printed in Canada.

Cover design: Steven Rosenberg

Some of these stories have appeared in *The Antigonish
Review, Border Crossings, Grain, Prairie Journal of
Canadian Literature, Scrivener,* and *Western Living.*

Canadian Cataloguing in Publication Data

Braun, Lois, 1949-
   A stone watermelon
   ISBN 0-88801-107-5
I. Title.
PS8553.R28S7 1986   C813'.54   C86-098081-2
PR9199.3.B72S7 1986

For my mother,
Dora Alberta Broeska

Contents

The Queen Passes By

The Queen was in the city. Alberta scythed masses of pink and white geraniums out of the windowbox with the long butcher knife she'd saved from the farm. She had never cared for flowers. John had always done all the gardening. But the windowbox had been there, and the man at the Safeway said their geraniums were on sale. The motorcade would glide past Jimmy's Deli and Lounge later today, the very place where Alberta spent her Sunday afternoons.

Every Sunday she dressed up in her navy funeral suit and went to Jimmy's for chicken salad and a martini. Her son had taken her there for Mother's Day shortly after she'd moved to the city, and because it was not a long drive from her apartment, she'd adopted the deli. Jimmy's had tall cathedral windows overlooking a small courtyard. When she looked into it, she saw her own orchard, which, like Jimmy's, had been leafy and bright in the summers, and a marble sculpture garden during the winter, when hoar-frost and snow thickened the branches of plum and apple trees. Alberta liked to sit in the window-light on Sundays at Jimmy's and watch all the people in their church clothes. And remember her orchard.

She carried the armful of geraniums through the living room to the little kitchen where she had a bowl ready with water. The plastic, imitation-crystal salad bowl had been left behind by the previous tenants. Alberta lowered her embrace of flowers into the water. "Well, Your Highness, they ain't all the same length." She took the knife and trimmed off the bottoms of the stems. The Queen was in the city. The geraniums were to be part of Alberta's private celebration, along with a bit of gold Christmas-tree garland she'd fished out of a box of ornaments. "I've seen you in pink before. Blue's your best, if you don't mind my saying so, but it don't give blue g'raniums. I don't think."

Alberta spoke to the old picture she had brought from the farm and propped up next to the unused toaster-oven her son had given her. The Queen and Prince Philip and Prince Charles and Princess Anne stood on a huge lawn. The Princess wore a mini-skirt. Even the Queen's knees were showing. "Your knees ain't the best," she'd been telling the Queen lately. She had seen a gold framed picture in a gift shop beside Jimmy's, a picture with the whole kaboodle, including Di. *Royal Souvenirs*, a sign in the window had said. But the new picture cost fifty dollars, more than Alberta could afford.

She looked at her watch. "Well, Your Highness, it's three weeks this time. 'Come to the city,' he says, 'so I can see you more often. You'll be too lonely on the farm.' Three weeks this time. Course, I don't suppose your Princes is real thick with you, neither."

It was seven-thirty a.m., perhaps already late if she was to have a spot right on the street. Alberta imagined the motorcade moving along the street, sleek, black metal slinking over grey pavement. She looked at the black ceramic panther on top of the TV in the living room, the long, narrow, shiny panther with the hole in its back full of fake ferns. Alberta had saved it from the farm, too. Thirty years ago, John's mother had handed it to her as a house-warming present, gift-wrapped, and whispered, "Now you look after my John, Girl, and no hanky-panky. And don't work him too hard."

Had the Sundays and evenings he'd spent carving her orchard been the "too much" the doctor had intoned across an empty white bed on the afternoon of John's death? She recalled another afternoon, one much further away. With her baby boy in her arms, she'd come home from the hospital to find a television set, decorated with the panther, squatting on the sloping floor of the sitting room, and John in his town clothes, beaming in the doorway. He'd turned a switch with a loud click and the first thing he and Alberta saw was the Queen with young Prince Charles. It was like a promise.

Alberta looked back at the picture. "Who do you talk to in your private moments, Highness?" and she placed the bowl of flowers in front of it.

Alberta put on the navy suit. Her husband had died in the summer, so that her funeral suit, though dark in colour, was lightweight and proper enough for the Queen. She added the pink scarf she'd found in the incinerator room yesterday. Then she put one sprig of pink geranium in a plastic breadbag with sprinkles of cool water. She opened her purse to make sure there were still a few dollars in the side pocket, and, with a lipstick tube she found among old shopping lists and wrinkled tissues, she made a few hasty dabs on her fading lips.

As she passed the incinerator room on her way down the corridor, she slowed down and then stopped just beyond the door. She'd salvaged many treasures from the incinerator room — a transistor radio that needed nothing more than new batteries and a polishing, two mugs that said GRANDMA and GRANDPA on their sides, an electric barbecue starter. Tenants put them on the table because such items were not allowed in the incinerator. Alberta had once seen a black ceramic panther just like hers on that table. But she hadn't taken it. What would she do with two? Such treasures were rare, though. Mostly she took magazines, which a certain thoughtful G.G. Felcher did not incinerate, but instead, placed them aside. Alberta decided not to enter the room now. She would do it later, before she cooked those sausages and potatoes for supper.

Outside, the air was bright and warm. The Queen only came in summer. Though it was not Sunday today, it felt like it, what with the suit and cordoned streets and the day-in-the-park sunshine.

Many people were already waiting and settled on lawn chairs on the sidewalk near Jimmy's when Alberta got there. Alberta had no chair. She couldn't stand for four hours, but she didn't want to go back home, and the deli didn't open until eleven, weekdays. She went back to her car and sat in it with the windows open. The next time I see him maybe I'll mention the picture, she thought. Aw, he hasn't got no extra cash, neither. Coming here sure don't make you rich.

She looked at the geranium through the words on the plastic. Breadcrumbs clung to the flaccid petals. Alberta started the car and turned on the air conditioner, then tucked the bag under the blast on the floor. She had gotten a nice car with the farm money. The rest of the money had gone to creditors. At least she could drive to town in style. She patted the seat.

How elegant it would be to sit in Jimmy's sculptured courtyard while waiting for the Queen! But the flower had to be fresh, and she couldn't just leave the car unattended with the air conditioner blowing on the geranium. That would mean leaving the key in the ignition, and there were so many strangers around today. "C'mon, Highness. It's been a long time and I'm hot. Let's get this show on the road, Girl."

At eleven o'clock Alberta locked up the car and made her way through the hot, sunburnt crowd lining the street, using her handbag as a shield for the geranium. But she had to walk two or three blocks before she could squeeze in front of a tall man wearing a sun visor. She was on the street. It was nearly time.

The first time the Queen had come to the city, John had appeared in the kitchen with his cap pushed back, one finger scratching the inside of his ear. "Things won't pan out for tomorrow, Allie. South wind today. We can start the barley tomorrow'n I need you to truck."

"Truck yourself," she'd said. "I'm going." And she had, in a car with a door that didn't close. She wired it shut as best she could and, with her son, found the Queen. Good thing she'd gone. She'd even touched the Queen's hand in front of the legislative building.

Alberta took the geranium out of the breadbag and dropped the bag on the ground. The shuffling feet of the crowd kicked the bag until it popped out onto the street. The street was a wind tunnel, with all the people thick-walled along its sides, and a gust of warm air pushed the breadbag along the pavement for several yards, directly ahead of a vanguard of men wearing dark three-piece suits and sunglasses. Security men, Alberta knew. "Mounties," she said to the man with the visor. "But I don't see no oozies." He didn't answer her, but reached down and picked up the little girl beside him. The child held a daisy in her hands. The man lifted her to his shoulder. No signs of a mother or more children.

"Don't throw it till you see her," said Alberta to the girl. "She won't be in the first car. I'll tell you when it's her."

Car-metal flashed behind the security guards. Sleek black cars passed with the warm wind. In them men with white teeth, women with big hats smiled and nodded. "Not them, not them," said Alberta.

The Queen was in a car with a glass roof, lit up by the sun. Her skin was the colour of a cat's ear. All down the line ahead of her, voices swelled. "It's her! It's her!"

"Get ready!" said Alberta. "Wait until she's looking right at you." She held the geranium at her breast. The Queen smiled and waved and said things to the others in the car, her lips moving in silent sentences. When she was even with Alberta and the tall man and the child, she looked at the people on the other side of the street and waved. Then, at the last possible moment, her head came around and she looked at the three of them. "Now!" Alberta cried, and she tossed the pink geranium towards the Queen's eyes. It struck the window and fell to the street. Directly behind it flew the daisy, though it did not touch the car. And now the two flowers lay side by side on the pavement.

More security men appeared, and policemen on motorcycles. It seemed very loud, suddenly, and Alberta was relieved when the sweating crowd began to break up. The man lowered the child to the ground and took her hand and began to walk away. "You're lucky," said Alberta, reaching down to pat the little girl's hair. "She'll remember you in her dreams."

The man gave the child a yank. "Don't touch the kid!" he growled. Alberta pulled her hand away as though the blonde hair had turned to worms. "Weirdo," he said to the child and towed her into the crowd.

Alberta's face flamed. It was too hot today. She unwound her scarf from her neck and opened the top button of her polyester blouse. With the pink scarf she dabbed at her forehead and under her eyes and at her chin. She felt so hot, but the scarf was dry. Weirdo! He couldn't have been talking about her. She looked into the faces of people pushing past her. He couldn't have meant her.

Blinds of Mexican cloth hung across Jimmy's windows. Alberta had claimed the last seat in the sun, only to have a satin-skinned waitress pull satin cords to blot it out. The blinds did not come all the way down, though, and Alberta's table-top remained in sunlight. The martini sparkled and flashed like a crown jewel. Alberta had two martinis — the Queen did not pass by every day. She was the only person sitting alone today, she noticed. Perhaps if she hadn't been alone when she touched the little girl's hair, the tall father wouldn't have been afraid of her. Alberta sipped at her martinis.

The streets were back to normal when she left Jimmy's, except for the litter of flowers crushed and blown, and flags dropped by tired children. It didn't feel like Sunday any more. "Bet you're back at your hotel with your feet up by now, Highness," Alberta muttered. Customers crowded the Royal Souvenirs shop. Through the plate glass door Alberta could see her picture still displayed on a peg-board wall. The Queen was in blue.

In the parking lot a large family funnelled into the back of a camper truck next to her car. When she backed out of her stall, small faces peered at her through the camper door. Alberta found her hand coming up. A royal wave.

As she came over the crest of a bridge she had to cross on the drive home, Alberta slowed down. Below her, the cars all swerved around something just where the road took a curve. When she came up to the object, she stopped the car, right in the middle of the street. It was a briefcase, black, rich-looking. Behind her, cars honked. Alberta shifted into Park and got out of the car. Holding her hand up above her head as a stop-sign, she hurried with short steps to the briefcase and rescued it from the street.

The leather was hot, too hot to touch. With the palm of her hand she tested its surface over and over again until she could rest her hand on the grainy leather. What could be inside? Maybe it was the oozies.

After the sunlight, the corridor was dimmer, bleaker, hotter. The apartment was just slightly cooler because Alberta had opened windows at opposite ends before she'd left. With her suit off, sitting in her slip in the kitchen, her stockings rolled down and her knees apart to cool the insides of her thighs, Alberta drank cold coffee and looked at the briefcase lying on the table.

The custodian had been in her apartment a few months ago to repair a corner of loose carpet in the living room. Alberta had been watching the Pope's visit to America on television. "See that guy with the briefcase?" Harv had asked, pointing with his hammer. "CIA. Know what's in the briefcase?" Alberta saw no one with a briefcase. "Oo-zies. In case of a terrorist attack. One of the boys always carries oozies."

To Alberta it sounded like bubblegum.

"Automatic sub-machine gun made in Is-reel. In split seconds they're ready to spray bullets." Harv whacked confidently at the carpet tacks. "Haven't you ever noticed the guy with the briefcase walking along with those motorcades? First thing I look for. Who's got the oozies. Say, you wouldn't happen to have a beer in your fridge, would you?" They had martinis.

Alberta had not seen a man with a briefcase walking alongside the Queen's motorcade. Even if there had been one, would he have dropped his oozy on the street? Still, she was afraid to open the briefcase and see the weapon. Perhaps it was locked.

Finally she put her thumbs on the locks, half-expecting them not to open at all. But they gave way easily. What if it was a gun? There'd be a reward, maybe a big one. Maybe fifty dollars. She would call the RCMP. They'd like that, probably even tell the Queen about it. She might want to see Alberta, to give her the reward in person and say thank you. Luckily, she already had a good suit.

The briefcase was filled with papers: letters and folders, and legal documents of some sort, with illegible signatures at the bottom. But stamped on all the papers, here and there, was one familiar name: Jimmy's Deli and Lounge. So. The briefcase belonged to Jimmy.

Alberta closed the briefcase. Jimmy was a rich man. The return of the papers would certainly be worth fifty dollars. Alberta rolled her stockings back up and put on a plain summer dress and lipstick and sandals.

"Well, Your Highness, there may be more chances for luck here, if you keep your eyes open and ain't afraid to grab for it. I can call up my boy and tell him about it and not have to beg for nothing. Maybe I'll even invite him for supper, show him my new picture and your geraniums there. Maybe he'll say, 'Naw, let's go out for a nice dinner.' Or maybe he's been laid off again, in which case he'll be stuck in a pub somewheres." Alberta hung her purse over her arm and picked up the black briefcase. "Sorry it wasn't Your Highness's oozy."

Too bad she hadn't worn the funeral suit. She would have felt as though she belonged with the three-piece men having cocktails and business talk, some with briefcases open on the low tables. Maybe she should go back home and mail the papers. Then she could keep the briefcase, to carry with her sometimes. Perhaps she could even put something in it. Pictures, or something. But the bartender was looking at her now. He was serving beer to the two men seated at the bar. He'd be the one to ask, because this was the room with the PRIVATE door at the back. Pin-striped backs of men often disappeared through that door when she sat at the window in the next room.

"Could I — ?" Her voice was a croak. She cleared her throat. The two men at the bar turned their heads to look at her. They both wore glasses and had expensive haircuts. Lawyers, she thought.

"Could I see the manager?"

The bartender's face became secretive. "May I tell him on what business?"

"Tell him it's about a briefcase."

The bartender went to the PRIVATE room and closed the door behind him. What would Jimmy look like? Tall, slim, blond, with a shy smile and a handsome face. When the door opened again, the bartender was preceded by a short squat man wearing a white shirt with the sleeves rolled up and the collar unbuttoned. A thick gold chain glinted at his throat. His mouth smiled at Alberta. "Yes, Ma'am. I understand you found my briefcase."

"Are you Jimmy?"

"My name is Harvey Goldberg. There is no Jimmy."

No Jimmy? Harvey? *Who's got the oozies.* "I found it in the middle of the street, just past the bridge. Everybody drove around it, but I stopped to pick it up before it got run over. I knew there might be something important in it." Alberta smiled at him with her mouth.

"Well, thanks a million. I appreciate your taking the time to pick it up. See, I put it on the roof of my car when I left here earlier today — while I looked for my keys — and I forgot it was there. I guess it slid off when I took the curve...."

"...I nearly got killed, but.... Well, here it is."

"I think I've seen you here before."

"Every Sunday. Every Sunday."

The lawyers were smiling, too. "Well, thanks — a lot," said Harvey again.

Alberta stood there, her eyes on the briefcase. "I was out front earlier today to see the Queen pass by. Were you there?" Over Harvey's shoulder she saw the bartender sneer.

Harvey waved his hand. "Are you kidding? I've got better things to do than wait for some old lady to smile at me through bullet-proof glass."

Alberta clutched her purse tighter to her stomach. The Queen was younger than she was!

"Uh — well, just hang on, uh — what's your name?" Harvey

closed one eye.

"Alberta." The croak again.

"Wait here, Mrs. Alberta." The lawyers whispered and laughed. Harvey took the briefcase to the PRIVATE room. Probably checking to make sure I didn't snitch anything, Alberta thought. What would I do with those papers, scribble on 'em with crayons? After a few minutes he came out and, with another smile for Alberta, passed through the lounge to the restaurant. Alberta smiled at the lawyers. They smiled at her and swallowed their beer.

When Harvey came back, he was carrying a small plastic container with a lid. Alberta recognized it: one of their deli take-out containers. "The waitresses tell me you like our chicken salad."

"Chicken salad?"

"Here. On the house. And thanks a million. Enjoy."

Chicken salad. The lawyers smiled.

Luckily, the page was clean. No rings from perspiring drink glasses, no food stains, no sweaty thumb prints. G.G. Felcher had been merciful. Alberta released it with careful tugging from its staples and placed it flat on top of the picture frame. Too big. A little too wide. "Your Highness, begging your forgiveness, I'll have to chop off some of your members." Alberta folded the page at each side to find out how much she'd need to cut away. If she trimmed off Andrew from one side and Edward from the other, the picture fit exactly into the frame and still left Charles. "Brats," she whispered to the new Queen. "I guess I could have left the picture just folded and they still would have been there, even if I couldn't see 'em." She held the magazine photo at arm's length. "Well, it's too late, Highness. At least, nobody's bony knees is showing, and I kept your dogs in."

Alberta wiped the arborite table to remove all traces of sausage grease before putting the picture in the frame. Her chicken salad reward sat alone on a curb in Jimmy's parking lot. She'd stood at the car and looked at the translucent plastic lid for a long time before putting it down on the curb. "Maybe someone'll take it home for their dog." She thought of the children in the camper. "He wouldn't have said that about you, Highness, if I hadn't been alone. If I'd had John with me, or a little granddaughter or grandson, or...."

She was about to remove the old photo from the frame when she remembered the layers of wallpaper she'd peeled away from the sitting room of the old house a long time ago. Leave the old one under the new. Coming home to that sitting room after touching the Queen's hand, she'd turned the television set on to watch film of the royal visit. She was still sitting there at dusk, her face blue in the glow of the black-and-white screen, when John came home. "How's the barley doin'?" she'd asked.

"Forty-five," he'd answered. "How's the Queen doin'?"

"We touched her."

Funny that Felcher put that *Life* magazine there just today. She looked at the telephone. "Maybe I'll give my prince a call tonight, tell him about it. You know, Highness, I wish he'd get married to a nice girl and have some kids. A couple of little girls with curly hair like his."

She would move the bowl of flowers and the gold tinsel and the picture to the television set in the living room. The Royal Visit Special would start at seven o'clock, according to the newspaper in the incinerator room.

There, it did fit perfectly.

But something was missing. Something that used to wave and bob in the corner of her eye when she sat at her table, something now missing and leaving a strange autumn feeling in the apartment. Alberta gazed at the windowbox with its headless plants. "And tell me, Highness, will them g'raniums bloom again?"

Three Crows Dancing

The sun moving north pointed shaming fingers at the breakfast cereal spattered on the south window above the kitchen table. The crusty brown specks had wintered there, not unnoticed, but uncared for. Now that it was April, full-scale window-cleaning would catch them at last.

Alice sprayed the whole window with cleaner from an aerosol can. The foam momentarily whitened the glass like the frost of winter. She decided to let the caked cereal soften a bit while she brushed Nora's fine blonde hair. When Alice went back to the window, the foam had deflated and dribbled down to the narrow sill and from there down the wall, as though rain had seeped through the glass.

"I make more mess cleaning...," Alice said to little Nora, who struggled with the aerosol can. The truth was, she'd known the foam would liquefy and run down the wall. But every day she waited for surprises. She passed an old undershirt of Walter's across the window. Now she could see Gypsy writhing in a dry patch of thin, dead grass on a high part of the lawn near the house. The cat flung her body this way and that, rolling and twisting and flailing her paws at the sun. Harry appeared at the far end of the low muddy driveway. The white jug in his left hand swung back and forth as he picked his way along the edge of the mud. Nora sprayed herself in the chest with window-cleaner. "Look!" cried Alice. "Here comes Harry with the milk. Run to the living room and see. He's walking today." She managed to seize the can from Nora before the child ran on her awkward short legs to the next room.

Alice had to finish the window and rub the wet stains off the wall before Harry saw them, or he would laugh. And her blanket and pillow were still on the sofa, and her nightgown crumpled on the coffee table, its yellow rosebuds shabby in the spring sun coming through the picture window. "Wave, Nora, wave to Harry!" She didn't have time to wipe the window-cleaner off the window-sill and the wall, *and* clear off the sofa. Today Harry would find out she didn't sleep in Walter's bed.

Alice's rag slid across the cracks between the window and the frame, between the frame and the wall, underneath the sill, cracks that Walter had brutally sealed with thick veins of caulking compound and which were now blackened with house dirt. Walter caulked everything that leaked. Mildewed veins encircled the bathroom faucets, the bathtub, the plumbing in the kitchen, doorframes, baseboards, and most of the windows. Whenever he felt a draft or suspected that moisture was infiltrating, he charged down the basement stairs as if to battle, and came back up with a loaded caulking gun, smug and sinister.

Walter had also banned Alice's sister, Mavis, from the house. She had reported Walter to the public health authorities for childbeating. But Walter was not a child-beater. It was just that he threatened and roared around so much that he'd convinced the witless Mavis he had beaten Nora, and Alice as well. And indeed, he had bludgeoned them so much with words that he may as well have driven his fists into their jaws.

The doorbell rang once and Harry came into the breezeway. Nora flitted through the kitchen to the stairs at the back entrance where he was taking off his shoes. "Morning, baby," said Harry. Alice heard him thunk the milk jug down on the step. Nora squealed in anticipation of Harry's tickling fingers. Alice pushed the kitchen table back in its place under the window and tossed the limp bit of undershirt over Nora's head towards the bathroom beyond. She hadn't balled it up tightly enough and it flared out as it flew and landed on the hallway floor, short of its mark. Harry's head popped around the corner at that moment. "Spring cleaning?" he asked.

He put the jug on the counter next to the fridge and teased Nora with the floppy fingers of his leather work-gloves while Alice poured new white milk into a plastic cup. Every morning the same: the new white milk in the kitchen with Harry and Nora, after Walter had rocketed off in his black Ranchero to speed around his vast acreage looking for trouble. While he spun about in angular, gravelled orbits, leaving trails of white dust behind him, Alice and Harry and Nora received the blessing of the fresh milk in a quiet kitchen. Then Alice would say, "Coffee?" or sometimes just hold out a cup and raise her eyebrows, and Harry would just nod, or sometimes answer by sitting down at the arborite table, always in the chair with the broken swivel, and wait for Alice to heat up cups of water in the microwave. They would sit and talk about Nora's teeth, about the burn Harry'd gotten on the inside of his leg from the exhaust pipe of his motorcycle, about the front steps shifting. And at the end, Harry would ask, "Did Walter say what he wanted me to do today?"

But this morning their eyes couldn't quite meet. It wasn't only Alice's bed-things in the living room. There was more.

"Rocky carries Gypsy's kitten around in his mouth as if she was a bone," said Harry.

"She'll get too big eventually."

"I don't trust Rocky. He'll chomp down on her all of a sudden. Or just plain worry her to death."

"Stop him then. Beat him when he does it."

"I'm not around enough."

"Me neither."

Harry looked at Nora when he spoke. Alice looked out of the window. Gypsy had folded herself up on the dry sunny spot to watch three crows dancing on the road.

"Did Walter say...?"

"No."

"...anything about you coming in late?"

"No. He was asleep." They'd smoked dope in Harry's parents' garage the night before and looked at April stars, and kissed. Their tongues had touched, and they kissed again. And then some more. And more. They'd stood on an oily cement floor kissing until it became pointless to carry on. Alice had walked home at midnight. Halfway there, she'd stopped and laughed out loud, just one short laugh that got Rocky barking and frightened a darkening rabbit out of the ditch. The dog may have awakened Walter. He knew Alice had gone to Harry's to return empty milk jugs and egg cartons. He probably thought she was drinking beer with Harry and his father. Safe.

Nora had gone into the hall and found the damp rag on the floor. She came into the kitchen with it, holding it up so that it dangled by one shoulder-strap from her short fingers. "Daddy," she said.

"Not any more," said Alice, laughing self-consciously. "Dirty." She took the rag and dabbed at a corner of the window with it to help Nora understand the transformation. The black Ranchero shot by and disappeared.

"I guess I better...." said Harry.

"No rush. He didn't say anything." Except, *Get the goddamn oatmeal off this window. This place is a pigsty. And I told you to shovel the friggin' mud out of the garage. It's practically up to my knees. Shit.* Alice could have turned on him and yelled that it didn't pay to shovel out the mud until the driveway had dried up, unless he decided not to park the Ranchero in the garage any more, but she kept her silence.

Walter had begun after she'd asked him for an apple tree. "I asked him for an apple tree this morning. For the front yard, so Nora could watch something grow, and so she could see blossoms in spring. He said, 'I can barely put food on the table. We don't need a thing like that.' And yet he goes all the way to Regina to buy an air conditioner for his Allis. He saves thirty dollars on the air conditioner and spends a hundred on gas and motel." She finally looked at Harry's face. "You'd buy your wife an apple tree, if you had one, wouldn't you?"

A crackling and breathing came from one corner of the kitchen counter. "Alice!" It was a bark. "Is Harry there yet? Alice?"

Alice reached for the talk-button on the two-way. "He's here."

The speaker snapped. "Tell him to get the flax. Horner wants it out of the way." A final click and silence.

"Get the flax. Horner wants it out of the way."

"Daddy," said Nora. She waddled into the living room.

"Why don't you get out of here, Alice?" Harry said, trying now to draw her eyes away from the patterns the milk was making in her coffee. He'd asked the question many times. She'd never answered.

Again, the static and the voice: "Tell him to replace the filters in the Allis. I'm going to Harley to look at that new discer." CLICK.

Alice watched the crows fly up and cross the road to the Klassens' pasture. Their black maple-twig feet dangled beneath them and their tattered wings beat slowly. Nora came back, laughing, with Alice's nightgown draped clownishly over her head. Harry picked her up and sat her on his knee. He played peek-a-boo with her among the folds of the nightgown. Alice felt embarrassed at first that Harry would smell her night smell in the limp, soft cloth. Then Nora was off again, leaving the nightgown on Harry's head. Alice picked it off and crumpled it in her lap. "How far away could I get? Everybody I know in the world lives here. If I could only get a little way away, would that do any good? I don't know if he needs me. He needs you, though. Don't think you can separate us but keep us each."

When Harry had left and Nora was snuggled in a bean-bag chair in front of the TV with her stuffed bulldog, Alice went to work on the accounts. Neat pencilled figures peered out at her from their linear cells in the debit columns like starving convicts. Walter had stopped looking at the accounts. He spent as little time as possible in the house. The winter had been a curious hell for them all, with his desperate scrabbling for reasons to spend long hours away from the house, and when he had nowhere to go he manoeuvred Nora roughly from room to room when she got in his way or made noise. He yelled at Alice about the house being a pigsty, about the refrigerator needing defrosting, about the laundry piling up, about the television being too loud. He could not stand a silence or a silence being broken. One warmish afternoon in January, Alice had bundled Nora up in a canary-yellow snowsuit and taken her out to the pond at the back of the yard. Alice scraped the snow off the ice with a big aluminum scoop and skated for Nora. She performed her clumsy figures on the warped, rough ice in a private bliss, remembering the roar and echo of the hockey arena in town where she'd taken lessons as a child, while Nora got cold in the snow-covered bank.

At noon, Alice closed the account book. The Ranchero appeared at the head of the driveway, and with scarcely a break in speed, it swerved and slithered up the muddy track towards the house. Walter refused the lunch she'd prepared—he'd eaten in Harley.

Alice saw justice sometimes. Shortly after her sister had broadcast Walter's atrocities, there was a nasty outbreak of grain weevils in Mavis's kitchen cupboards. She was squeamish about such soundless infestation, and begged Alice to come to her house to help poke about in cereal boxes and pancake mix and flour bags, and to vacuum all the shelves. Alice squatted smugly for hours in front of the lower cabinets, and pulled out jars and pots and packages of rice and macaroni that fairly throbbed with tiny brown insects, while her sister cowered over the sink sanitizing all the dishes. Later she handed Alice ten dollars with a pale, prunish hand. Alice accepted it without protest.

Alice roamed about the yard, tugging at the dead underbrush among the lilac clumps and catoneasters. She stamped her rubber boots on stubborn snow-heaps on the north side of the yard so that they'd melt and disappear more quickly. Her boots clogged with mud in the low places and she wished May would hurry up so that she could find some real work to do, prepare seed-beds, rake up the nap of the lawn in front of the house, collect dead-fall from the shelter belt. This vagrancy was wearing down her ambition — she was not content inside the house or out of it. The ruts on the driveway turned grey at the upper edges as they began to dry, but at the same time there was an odd blueness in the west, a sultry heavy darkness that at this time of year could mean rain or snow. Alice looked at the clouds through a brambly old lilac row and saw Walter and Rocky walking between the bright red granaries beyond the garden. Rocky was worrying the kitten, picking her up in his mouth, dropping her, pinning her down with his clumsy mud-encrusted paw. Walter leaned down and scratched Rocky behind his right ear.

It rained. Alice and Nora came home during the downpour, after shopping in town. They parked the old station wagon on the road and left the groceries in it. Then the two of them scampered like wet mice up the driveway, dodging water-filled ruts and soft mounds of mud. Alice carried Nora part of the way. The torrent worsened after they got inside. Walter was not there. Once they'd towelled their faces and changed into fleece-lined sweatsuits, they sat cocooned at the kitchen table and watched the grey rain through the window. Alice thought about the roof. Though the house was not old, the roof leaked, and during heavy rains, water squeezed through the light fixture on the kitchen ceiling and tapped a slow telegraphic message on the linoleum. She looked up at the fixture now, half afraid she'd see the glitter of stealthy wetness forming around the edge of the metal plate riveted to the ceiling. It was dry. Walter had caulked it.

SNAP. "Alice!"

"Yes."

"Where were you? I've been calling all afternoon, damn you!"

"I did the shopping. Just got back. We're soaked...."

"Where's Harry?"

The breezeway door that led to the back yard opened. He'd run over from the machine shop.

"I don't know."

Walter's swearing blended with the static on the radio. Nora cooed at Harry in the breezeway. "I hit the ditch a little ways north of Krahns'. Find Harry."

Alice was about to say, "Are you okay?" but the radio clicked off.

"What'd he want?" Harry came into the kitchen, his hair and face dry because he'd been wearing his John Deere cap. The heavy woollen socks on his feet extended beyond his toes.

"He called to say he loves me."

"Nora's got a big bruise on her arm."

"How do you know?"

"I saw it this morning when I brought the milk."

"Rocky nipped her the other day. He was just playing."

"It's easier to forgive a dog, isn't it?" They were very careful not to touch each other. "I came to see if the roof was leaking."

"I suppose the roof is still leaking. Walter caulked the ceiling, though."

"We've got to fix that up before seeding. It's all rotting up there."

Alice shifted from foot to foot and finally lit a cigarette. The rain continued. She wondered when the two-way would sputter again.

"You're right, Alice. All you can see through this window is the road. My mom does nothing except watch the traffic going by all day long. I don't want you to end up like that." Harry pulled some bills out of his jeans pocket as though he'd had them ready for her. "Tell him you won it in one of those sweepstakes contests you're always entering." They laughed, because he had given her only a few dollars.

"I was hoping to win a cruise along the Rhine River."

"Get a tree first. You can keep a little back from your grocery money, can't you?"

"Does planting a tree mean I'll stay here forever?" Alice stared at the money.

Harry went to the breezeway to put his boots back on. "I'm gonna find Pete and go to the pub, try and forget it's raining." He ran back into the rain and Alice watched him skitter among the puddles.

"Take me with you," she whispered.

"Alice!"

"Walter, it was just starting to dry up and now it's going to be all soggy...."

"Alice, for shit's sake, I'm sick of sitting here looking out the windshield at the goddamn rain! Is Harry coming?"

"He's at the bar. I'll come with the Allis."

She took Nora to the Klassens' across the road and retrieved the groceries from the car. Then she went to look for a chain.

Walter's shop was tidy. Even before she snapped on the lights, Alice could feel the hard presence of his farm tools arranged around the perimeter of the steel building — welding equipment in one corner; propane torches, power drills, clamps, vises, saws and wrenches hanging above the workbench; axes, spades, pulley belts suspended from thick nails hammered into the wooden ribs of the structure. Her plastic rain cape bound her arms as she reached up to unhook a heavy tow chain hanging on the wall. As it came free, its dead weight pulled unexpectedly on her shoulders and its links hitting the floor rang out and echoed in the hollow space. Turning towards the door, her forearms draped with the chain, she saw Rocky silhouetted against the mist outside. He was black and still and watching her. Alice felt like a thief. She took a clevis from another hook near the door and, slinging the chain over her shoulder, hurried to the tractor in front of the shop.

The Allis drowned out the sound of the rain. Its wheels smashed through the mud and tossed up spongy clods as it bullied its way along the slippery road. Alice shivered inside the cab and fumbled for the heater switch.

She had to drive on three or four different roads to get to where Walter was. The roads were not all the same. One was hard in the tracks, one was little travelled and soft, one had just been gravelled and crunched even in the rain. On the last road Alice saw the Krahn farm a quarter-of-a-mile north. Beyond that somewhere was the foundered Ranchero. She began to sing one of Nora's lullabies, loud above the tractor engine:

Night seems darkest just before the dawn,
Just as the day-break nears.
Soon we'll see a sunny sky
It's time to dry your tears.

It was a song that Harry's father, the only man she knew who'd ever been to war, often sang when he'd been drinking beer. Alice sang it for Nora every evening and sometimes in the afternoons.

Somewhere the sun is shining
So honey don't you cry.
We'll find a silver lining,
The clouds will soon roll by.

She sped up as she passed the little white farmyard. A half mile further she saw the black mass in the ditch on her left side. Walter had been forced to sell his four-wheel-drive pick-up in the fall to make payments on fertilizer. He and Harry had found the Ranchero in a widow's garage on the outskirts of Harley, abandoned by its owner, her son and only child who had gone to Alberta to get rich. "Vent to Al-BAIR-ta," she had told Harry over the chipped rim of a dainty teacup. Walter and Harry had spent the last warmish days of November making the Ranchero driveable.

But now as Alice got near the truck in the steep watery ditch, she could see that its smeared windows were blank. Walter was not there. She'd expected to see his hatchet face glowering at her through the windshield, his knuckles white on the steering wheel, his teeth clenched, lower lip peeled away and curled down to his chin. She put the tractor in neutral as it came even with the truck and opened the door of the cab. She stood and leaned out towards the Ranchero. All she heard was the swish of rain on the winter-brown grasses and on the water in the ditch.

She slammed the door shut and sat down on the cold vinyl seat. Walter might have walked to Krahns' or been picked up by a passer-by and taken home by a different road, but Alice felt cheated and refused to resort to common sense. The road before her was straight and she decided to keep going. She was glad she'd learned how to drive the Allis. Before Nora had been born, she'd worked on the fields during the busy seasons, harrowing in the spring, trucking during harvest, tilling in the fall. It was lonely during busy seasons, when Walter and Harry were gone from sunrise to midnight, or later, day after day, week after week, and Harry's milk stops were short and business-like. Alice hadn't helped much with field work the last two years. Today she wanted to drive.

The rain was a drizzle now. Alice came to another gravel road and turned west. The land was flat around her with small lakes in the low parts of the fields. Shelter belts defining the farmyards that fronted the road were still partially filled with scruffy-looking snow. No one was about on the farms. They'd all been imprisoned by the mud and the rain. In some yards, sodden mongrels plodded between barn and house, late-afternoon hunger compelling them to test the air for the smells of cooking food.

Alice hummed her lullaby. She'd put on a pair of ear-protectors to cut the blare of the engine and her voice resonated between her throat and the centre of her forehead. All roads here were level and straight as rails. No dips into valleys, no hairpinning up steep grades, no twists around hills or villages, few correction lines. On some of the narrower ones, poplar trees stood tall and thick-trunked on either side, their upper branches spraying upward and outward to form a lofty arch above the roadbed. And beyond all the linearity, Alice knew, was the escarpment, where the roads took on mystery and illusion as they curved up the hill, shrouded by oak and maple.

> *You can't laugh until you've learned to cry,*
> *Sunshine must follow gloom.*
> *Life is filled with April show'rs*
> *To make the flowers bloom.*

Alice let the lullaby fill her mind, mile after mile, wiping away conscious thought like a ball of fleece. Then, passing through a long tunnel of arching poplar branches, she began to imagine the trees in blossom. The blossoms drifted down and surrounded the Allis. They lay white among roadside grasses and melted on the tractor cowling. The air had turned cold. The drizzle in its dying had been reincarnated as a spring snow, and Alice wondered if the snow would find Walter.

She looked at the fuel gauge. She had not filled the tank before leaving. A bit of sun seeped through a thin spot in the clouds. Behind her, the tractor tires left parallel wounds in the muddy road.

When Alice walked into the house, she could hear the two-way snapping and Walter's voice drilling into the quiet kitchen.

"Have you got enough?"

"More than enough. They don't cost nearly as much as I thought. I have to keep the money in Nora's piggy bank. He goes through my purse sometimes and takes whatever he finds."

"Gypsy's pregnant again...."

"I think we should stop."

"Stop?"

"Until I know what will happen."

"You'll never know what will happen. Happening is all the time. Happening was yesterday and right now. You have to put it together."

"But I think we could stop now. Just stop. Next week or next month might be too late, Harry."

"I love you, Alice."

"I don't...."

It was May. Seeding had begun, now that it was dry. It was so dry that dust from the escarpment, where they'd had fewer April rains, billowed into the lowlands on windy days and weakened the sun. But it was warm enough now to plant things. It was warm enough to plant an apple tree.

On a calm, clear morning flocked with willow buds, Alice went to the greenhouse in town. She carried Nora so that the child could see above the tops of the trestle-tables crowded with jewel-like blooms. Alice loved the greenhouse in spring. She couldn't buy much, but she liked the smells of chlorophyll and wet soil and nicotiana flowers. Nora's fine hair snagged in the ferns hanging from the rafters as Alice floated down the narrow aisles and feasted her eyes on sweet william and marigolds. A thin man pulled tiny weeds out of a bed of petunias. His face was colourless and he had long crinkly hair and a long beard. He reminded Alice of a weed that had sprouted under a board left lying on the ground. "We'd like to buy an apple tree."

The man was shy. He didn't say anything but led them to a corral outside that was full of young trees and shrubs, and Alice began reading tags. "Do you want one with real apples?" asked the weedy man.

"Real? I...."

"These trees over here have real pretty leaves and flowers, big ones, but they give fake apples."

"Fake?"

"Well, they look nice on the tree in winter, and the birds eat them. But people can't. Now, those trees have good eating apples, but their blossoms and leaves aren't quite as fancy."

"I think...."

"Apples or blossoms?"

"Apples. We want to eat them."

When she got home, she hid the tree behind the washing machine in the basement.

"Alice! Are you there? Alice!" He had gone out at five that morning to finish the wheat.

"Walter, I bought an apple tree yesterday. I'm going to plant it in the front yard."

"It won't grow! The soil is crappy there and it's always dry because it's higher. It'll just wither up. Bring me some breakfast." CLICK.

"I'll water it," said Alice.

"Water," said Nora.

Alice decided to plant the tree before she took Walter his breakfast. She stood at the kitchen window and then at the living room window, looking out at the patchy lawn in front of the house. Where should the apple tree be planted? She got it from the basement and took it out onto the lawn. Then she went back into the house and stood at the windows again. She moved it around three more times until she had determined the spot.

Walter's machine shop was in confusion now that it was seeding time. Socket wrenches, screwdrivers, greaseguns were flung about on either side of a space that had held the Allis earlier that morning. They gleamed sullenly at her as she looked for a spade. Her foot caught on the cord of a trouble-lamp that lay on the oil-stained floor where Walter had used it for making repairs. It slid along the concrete. The sound reverberated around her and she heard Gypsy call out from among pails and rags and empty cartons underneath the workbench where she'd delivered her kittens a week ago. The spade was still in its normal place.

Alice began to dig into the roots of grass at the spot she had chosen. Maybe Walter had been right — the ground was almost too hard to dig into. She pushed as hard as she could on the shoulder of the spade but was able to tear up only small bits of root and earth. She moved to a less grassy area of the lawn, but the dirt was hard there, too. She threw off her sweater and kept at it, but seemed to get nowhere. *It won't grow. It'll just wither up.* Her hair fell into her eyes as she struggled. Through it, she saw Rocky coming towards her with something in his mouth. One of Gypsy's kittens.

It was dead.

At first, Alice hit the dog only with the flat bottom of the spade. She hit him over and over again on his back and rump. Why doesn't he run?

But Rocky stayed, with his tail between his legs and his ears down. He kept twisting around to face her.

She turned the spade and beat him with the sharp edge of it. He began to whimper and cower. Nora was crying.

"Alice! Alice!" Harry ran up the driveway with the milk jug bobbing at his side. "Stop it, Alice!" But she continued to slash at Rocky's black flesh, watching wounds open and blood begin to ooze.

Run, she thought. Run, run....

Harry dropped the milk and dove for the shovel just as Alice was about to strike Rocky between his flattened ears. Alice dropped to the ground. She sobbed, her tears mingling with sweat.

"The kitten was already dead, Alice," Harry panted as he cradled her head in his arms. "Rocky didn't kill the kitten. It was lying dead beside the workbench when I came back from the field late last night, probably sick. I was too tired to throw it in the pond." He pushed the hair away from Alice's eyes. "Dumb dog must have found it early this morning when Walter was working in there. Rocky didn't kill it."

"Why didn't he run?"

Nora stopped crying and looked at the milk jug on its side on the driveway. The top had come off and milk trickled among the pebbles and soaked into the ground. "Spill," she said.

"Walter could shoot it with his gun," said Alice. "But it's too late, isn't it, Harry?"

The tender young leaves of the apple tree began to flicker in a breeze that had come up out of the southwest. "Spill," said Nora again.

"Spill," said Alice.

Golden Eggs

A bump and giggle meant the girls were up. Two for sure, probably
Moses and Violet, who slept side by side in a single cot at the head
of the stairs. Every morning they awoke with the first rasp of the
pump beside the kitchen sink and then quarrelled in whispers
under the comforter.

Sarah let her hand rest on top of the woodstove for a moment,
feeling it heat up as the oak kindling started to crackle and hiss.
Summer was over now. In one night, the weather had turned
almost winter-cold. Her girls would need their coats and stockings
this morning. She was lucky, they'd needed only sweaters all
September, though she had seen them squatting in their skirts on
the street, after the sun had gone down, to keep their bare legs
warm.

Bare feet padded on the cold upstairs floor. A balled-up pair of
brown wool stockings bounced down the steep staircase, and after
it, Violet, wearing a man's suit jacket over her nightgown. She
fished the stockings from under the chair with no back and rolled
them up to her ankles. "Can I cut the bread?"

Sarah threw the knife down beside the bread on the wooden
table and turned her back on it, but then regretted her surliness.

Violet always came down the earliest and cut the bread the straightest. Sometimes she peeled the potatoes or helped Betty-Ann get dressed. But mostly she liked to tell stories, stories from thick books she read at school, about hags and genies with hair as long as ladders. She painted the stories in thrilling colours and textures for her cloistered listeners. Violet's teacher was a girl from across the river where they had no religion. At first Sarah worried that the stories might be heathen. And then, her worry became guilt when she realized she enjoyed the flow of glass coffins and castle towers and magic kisses and dogs with eyes like saucers. Not that lions' dens and fiery furnaces weren't picturesque enough. It was just that her father had imparted all Bible stories with solemn reproach, with the burden of Old Testament sin heavy in his voice. Every villain was the Devil.

Sarah popped a slice of raw potato into Violet's mouth and said, "Have they started fighting yet?" Over the stockings. There were never enough whole stockings on any chilly morning. Knitting as fast as she could, Sarah could not keep up with the girls' toes and heels bursting through the brown wool. And they were often one pair short. She wished for the magic spinning wheel from Violet's story.

"Not yet. They don't know how cold it is." Violet measured the slices with her eye before cutting into the new loaf. "Except Bowlie. She slept with hers on. Scratch came to the yard yesterday and told her secretly that it was going to get terrible cold overnight. Don't ask me how he knew." Bowlie wore her stockings night and day all winter long. When they got holes, she'd get up after her sisters had fallen asleep at night and ransack the bottom bureau drawer for the newest pair, replacing them with her holey ones. So the sisters made fun of her bowed legs, and told their friends at school that she was "bowl-egged." Bowlie didn't care. She was an odd, self-contained child who had formed a curious bond with the skinny, ragged boy they called Scratch. Most of the townspeople thought Scratch was a demon, but both Sarah and Bowlie respected his omniscience.

"Anybody sick today?"

"No. Lulu's crying as usual."

More bumps from above. This time with whimpering and sniffling. Lulu always cried in the morning because her bed-partners pinched her to get her awake.

Sarah pumped water into a basin and carried it to the tiny bathroom at the back of the house where the older girls washed and put on their lipstick. A calendar with a kitten on it hung on the bathroom wall. September had been torn off. Ben's letter said he'd be coming home on the train around the fifteenth. It had been over nine months since her husband had been home. He'd arrived a few days after Christmas, complaining that his work had kept him back. Sarah didn't believe that the Alberta oil company he worked for had its men working on Christmas Day. His delay had only inflated the girls' excitement, and when he'd shown up with silk stockings for Alma and Esther and Katherine, and fur muffs for the young ones, they'd taken turns sitting on his lap for the rest of the evening. Except for little Betty-Ann, who didn't recognize her father. He would bring gifts now, too, but would leave again before Christmas. This year the girls would have to be satisfied with nuts and candy and home-made mittens and tams.

When Sarah came back into the kitchen, Violet was trimming the crusts from one of the bread slices. She had carved them into neat squares and triangles and circles and arranged them in a pattern on the table. All was play to her. Why couldn't she, Sarah, have learned such play as a child? Her father had enslaved her as soon as she could pump well-water and learn Bible verses, and now Ben, who soldiered in foreign lands, could not endure the confines of her small life.

Sarah's anger rose again like boiling milk. "Violet, I told you not to cut the crusts off the bread!"

"Just one, Mama! Lisa always leaves hers over anyhow. Might as well cut them off ahead of time."

"I always eat Lisa's crusts!"

"Well, here then." Violet jumbled the little collage in her hands and held them out to her mother.

Sarah wanted to grab Violet's fists and squeeze until her fingers opened and the crusts fell to the floor. But instead, she gestured to the shelf beside the sink and said, "Put them in my cup. I'll soak them in my coffee. And bring me the plates."

They heard the train whistle just as the sun made a starburst on the gilded rim of the teacup Ben had given Sarah for Christmas. It sat unused on the sill of the window above the sink. Sarah was at the stove, stirring a mixture of potatoes and lard and water in two big black skillets. When she heard the whistle, she stopped and looked at the window. Violet was there, washing herself. The child bent her dripping face towards the gold star at the teacup's edge, then held a wet hand in the sunbeam to see if the light would make stars on the droplets suspended from her fingertips.

Sarah went back to her stirring. Violet dried her face. "When's Daddy coming?"

Sarah hadn't told anyone about the letter, but they always started asking about their father just before he came home. "Soon." She went to the foot of the stairs and called, "Girls!"

The last time Ben was home, Sarah had tried to get him to sleep on the decrepit sofa in an alcove just off the kitchen. Betty-Ann was used to sleeping with her in the double bed in the back room of the tiny house, she said, and the little girl couldn't be expected to sleep alone in a space she wasn't used to. But Ben had given Betty-Ann a bright new nickel and she became an easy traitor to her mother. By pure luck, Sarah had not become pregnant last time Ben had been home, nor the two times before that. She didn't plan to, ever again.

For twenty-six years he'd been leaving her in this shack while he spent long months on jobs in far-away places, coming back on the train only long enough to make her pregnant and put stars in his daughters' eyes. They'd had two sons as well as the twelve girls: the first- and second-born had been boys. As soon as they were old enough, their father had found them work with the oil company, and now Sarah saw them less often than she saw Ben. The boys didn't like coming home to a crowded house filled with girls.

Take me, Ben. Take me this time. Sarah put her hand to the tight knot of hair at the back of her neck, a smooth, petrified knot that was out of her sight during the long days, but became in the mirror at night a girlish auburn spill of light on her breast. When he was home, she turned out the lamp before he could see it.

Looking at the sofa now, Sarah wondered how she might engineer her husband to sleep on it this time. Perhaps now that the lumps and sags were out of it.... In May she had gone to see Kaminsky, the storekeeper, who also sold and repaired furniture. Kaminsky was bald and had tufts for eyebrows. He reminded Sarah of the genie in Violet's book.

"How much to have that old red sofa of mine restuffed?"

"Five dollars, if you want new springs."

Five! That took a big chunk out of grocery money. Violet kept pennies in a cigar box....

"Two for stuffing and my time."

"Forget the springs. Who needs springs?"

A few days later, he was at her door with an enormous sack on his shoulder. While she ironed little cotton dresses, he pulled old clothes, perfectly wearable old clothes, and straw out of the sack, and crammed them into the seat and back of the couch.

Unlike the other merchants in town, who were too friendly and traded their gossip for your business, Kaminsky was a haughty, cold man. His eyes narrowed when she gave him the two dollars, but he'd hardly said a word all afternoon. When he left, after sewing up the seams with a huge needle, Sarah felt as though she'd had a divine visitation.

There was a large thump and a wail from the upstairs room, and an impatient banging of drawers. "Girls!" Sarah called again. She could hear another muffled thumping somewhere, at first she thought in the cellar. "The devil's at the door," she muttered to herself. But then she realized it was coming from the closet under the stairs. Violet was in there looking for the coats, probably intending to get the best one before her sisters came down. She emerged wearing a pretty one that was much too big for her. "There are only eight," she announced, with two or three draped over her arm.

"There are some in my bedroom closet."

"Teacher told us a story yesterday," said Violet as she and Sarah sorted through the eight coats in the narrow passageway between the kitchen and the back rooms. "It was about a fish that could talk. It was quite —" she paused, her hand in one of the coat pockets, "— smashing," she said, as though she'd found the word in the pocket. "It was about this fisherman and his wife who were very, very poor and lived in a horrible old shack.

"One day the man meets a fish in the ocean who — well, he doesn't meet the fish, he catches it, and then the fish says — I think the fish was beautiful with gold scales — the fish says, 'If you let me go, I'll grant you a wish.' " Violet crossed her eyes and changed her voice so that it sounded bubbly. Sarah scratched at a spot on one of the coats and tried not to laugh. "So the man did it. Moses says it was stupid for the man to believe that a fish could grant wishes, but I said that if a fish could talk — I mean, talk English — then it was ob'iously magic." Moses was a pious, practical, old-womanish child and therefore Violet's opposite. Moses never went anywhere without her tree-branch walking staff, and on Sundays, a Bible under her arm. Her real name was Rose.

"So the man asks his wife what to wish for and she tells him to wish for a new cottage. The man goes back to the ocean and asks for a new cottage. Well, first he has to say this little poem. And when he gets home, there it is, a new cottage with his wife in it. But she keeps sending him back to ask for more and more, and finally they live in a huge castle. Pretty soon the wife says she wants to be the lord of the sun and the moon, and when the man tells the fish, the fish says, 'Go home,' like always, and when the man goes home, it's a shack again."

"You'll have to let Anna have that coat, Violet. It doesn't fit you."

"But you know what, Mama? The man goes back to the beach one day and he finds the fish dead on the shore and he cuts it open with his knife and you know what he sees?"

"Guts."

"No. A golden egg!"

"Violet, you made that up. Last week you told me about cutting a goose open to look for golden eggs."

"Well—I felt sorry for him." The train whistle blew again, on the track at the other end of town.

One by one the girls came into the kitchen to wash at the sink and eat their mushy, salty potatoes and bread smeared with lard. Once they were all down, Violet, who never ate breakfast, went upstairs to dress, so she could have the dresser mirror to herself. She took a coat with her. Betty-Ann, cheeks shiny with warm lard, followed her up to explore the many perfume- and urine-scented beds.

"When's Daddy coming?"

"Soon." THWACK! The wooden spoon hit the bottom of each plate as Sarah measured out the potatoes. She had never gone anywhere with Ben on the train. He'd whisked Joseph and young Ben away on the train, and the older girls had all, at some time or other, stolen a trip to Winnipeg in a boxcar. Last spring, a rumour had trickled down the street that Anna had given her favours to the brakeman in return for a ride up front in the engine. Sarah hadn't been on the train since the time she was thirteen when her own mother had taken her to the city to escape from a smallpox epidemic. How many trains would it take to get to the ocean? These days, Sarah got only as far as Emerson and St. Joe, when the neighbours took her visiting in their Packard. She never went away for very long. It seemed dangerous to leave the house bristling with twelve females.

One by one, the children finished their breakfasts, and after Sarah had inspected their clothing for stains and torn seams, the younger ones scampered to the bathroom to have their hair braided by Katherine and Esther. Sarah herself brushed Lulu's curls. When she was about two, Lulu had smashed her head against a red-hot stove-pipe one bitter evening when her sisters had taken turns tossing her around the kitchen. Her hair had never grown back there. Sarah made sure every morning that the scar was well covered. "What about the stockings?" she whispered in Lulu's ear so as not to open that can of worms.

"One is missing," Lulu whispered back. "Alma only had enough for one leg."

"Did she cut it in half?"

"No. She's wearing her Daddy-stockings." Usually, only Katherine and Esther wore their silk stockings because they had jobs and were both engaged to be married.

"I'll knit like the devil tonight."

A kind of frenzy built up in the kitchen now, with everyone fed and dressed and invigorated by the prospect of the splash of cold air, everyone ready to fly from the house like so many jaunty balloons. But Sarah, who was at the counter beside the sink sliding puffy bits of leftover potatoes into another plate, her plate, had floated out into an ocean brimming with magic fish. She was the fisherman, not the old wife in the horrible shack, and there was a promise of golden eggs in the ocean's bright surface. At her elbow, the cool, scummy water in the sink rippled with the thumps and footsteps of the children behind her. Ripples in her ocean.

"Mama, there aren't enough coats." Violet stood just at the entrance to the passageway across the room. Her words rose above the other voices.

Who...? There was Bowlie, sitting on the old sofa, looking as though she would gladly walk across town to school with no coat on, if that's how things would end up. She wore her favourite short-sleeved floral-print dress and neat brown stockings. The other girls were dressed in wool coats of navy, dark green, black, chocolate, maroon. Katherine had bought her own coat last winter. She tied a yellow scarf around her neck and left the house.

Sarah's bedroom was dark and cold and peaceful. The privacy of the closet was seductive. Several times over the years she'd been startled when, after the chaos of getting everyone to bed, she'd opened the door to hang up her dress and found a daughter huddled inside, clutching a doll or sucking on a chicken bone.

Three coats hung in the closet, hers, and two very small coats that were big enough only for Molly and Betty-Ann, who didn't go to school yet.

Sarah went back to the kitchen. When she arrived empty-handed, the children fell silent. Then the younger ones began to hurry, in case they should somehow lose the coats they were already wearing. Violet said, "Mama, if you would let Alma or Esther wear your coat just for today, we would have enough."

Sarah stared at Bowlie on the sofa. *Give up her own coat?* "What about tomorrow? I don't have enough money to buy a coat for tomorrow. So what good would it do? Besides, my coat is a big, black, fat coat. People would think the devil had come to town."

"We can borrow one tonight. Just give us yours for today."

"We will not borrow clothes from our neighbours! I need my coat! I—have to go to buy wool for stockings. And I have to go to the post office. There might be—there might be a letter from your father."

"You could go to the post office after we get home from school."

"I will not be stuck here without my coat!" Sarah was answering Violet, but she was talking to Bowlie, who still sat on the sofa. Lulu and Molly began to cry.

"Well, what can we do then?"

Bowlie did not cry. She was a peaceful flower patch against a nubby red background.

Sarah picked up the breadknife still lying in a bedlam of crumbs on the breakfast table. "There will be enough coats."

With her left hand, Sarah pushed Bowlie off the sofa, and with her right, she plunged the knife into the seam in the middle of the back-rest. She hacked away at the red cloth until straw and stuffing bulged through the gash. No golden eggs, no emeralds or crowns, not even a piece of silk. What riches would she receive for rescuing Bowlie from the simple cold of an autumn morning? Sarah reached in and pulled out musty-smelling pieces of cotton and chintz and felt, frayed shirts, half-skirts, dress-sleeves, patched trousers. The large eyes of her children glowed at their mother's sudden wizardry. Closer they came and closer as the treasure chest spilled remnants of strangers' lives.

At last Sarah pulled out a green wool bundle that, when shaken out, looked like a coat.

"It's all wrinkled," said Moses in her low, old-woman voice.

Sarah held it up to Bowlie's shoulders. "Maybe a little small, but it will do until your father comes home with the money."

While the girls draped themselves in patchworks of cloth remnants, a paisley dress-sleeve here, a tweed pant-leg there, Sarah pulled the ironing board out of a cupboard and lifted one of the sad-irons from the stove. Violet picked straw off the new old coat.

"It just came to me that it was there," Sarah said to herself as she ran the iron along the green fabric. "It's funny how a person remembers things she thought she didn't ever know."

In twos and threes, the girls left the house and shouted down the street and to the new cold air. At the front of the yard, Scratch leaned against a maple tree, smoking a cigarette butt he'd found on the street. Soon only Violet and Bowlie remained in the kitchen.

"He brings us fancy teacups as though we were princesses living in a castle." Sarah's iron thumped on the board and she plucked at wisps of straw caught in the weave. Bowlie and Violet day-dreamed at the table with their chins in their hands.

At last Bowlie put the coat on. A button was missing and the sleeves did not quite touch the bones of her thin wrists. She opened the kitchen door and stood in the cold air for a moment, and watched Scratch puff on the stubby cigarette.

"What's for supper?" asked Violet.

"Fish."

"If they talk, listen."

Sarah went to the window to see the girls leave the yard. The glass was steamed up now and she had to wipe the moisture away with her hand. In a month or so, a layer of ice would coat the window, and she would have to press a hot iron to it to melt it away so she could look out while washing the plates.

The sun was higher and brighter now, and Sarah could see a piece of straw shining in Bowlie's dark hair. The other daughters were strung along the road like coloured wooden beads. All wore their brown woollen stockings. Violet walked by herself at the end, her head tilted up to catch the sunlight on her face. Her coat, a little too long, flapped at her knees. The whistle blew one last time as the train took on water before floating back into the clouds.

The Maltese Mistress

She looked out from a tropical darkness, her face glowed with a light that could have been from a beach fire or a lantern. Her hair was visible only at the profile of her forehead, the rest was melted into the night. She was looking over her shoulder. The expression on her face was neither amiable nor hostile, not one of surprise or admonition. But there was anger in it, everyone agreed. Her lower lip was poised as though she may have just begun to speak — there was ever so slight a parting of the lips, a tension at the corners of her mouth. On her bare shoulders you more imagined than actually saw a lustre of ocean waters, because her sleek appearance suggested that she had come out of the sea. Her hand, barely discernible, was held high against her chest, and clutched some sort of object. Some thought it was the handle of a knife, others believed it to be a piece of driftwood. A star-shaped blur of white in the background might have been a milky-coloured flower.

The portrait had stood propped up for almost a year against a row of dusty whisky decanters. Now, it hung on the wall behind the bar in this flat, badger-like prairie tavern, keeping company with the usual clutter of bar trappings, along with a mounted rabbit's head and a calendar featuring provocative photographs of pigs.

Though the only light in the establishment came from a collection of neon-bright electric clocks, the eyes in the portrait commanded first attention, even before the glass orbs in the jack-rabbit's skull. The sea-woman's eyes snapped with an energy the tavern's patrons seldom found in one another's.

Ben Champion and Julian Manness sat at the bar with one stool between them and looked straight ahead over their beer bottles, not at the rows and rows of liquor, or the portrait, or the calendar, but at memories of the past and mysterious clouds of future, which were supposed to meet now, and fit, and take on some sort of meaning, because Julian was going away. Mona, the bartender, sat opposite, facing them but not looking at them. They could do this, face each other comfortably for long hours without seeing. She smoked. Ben and Julian scratched at the foil labels on their bottles with their thumb-nails, making slender paths through the paper and glue, while their tongues stiffened against the roofs of their mouths. Julian had just returned from the East, from an orientation conference, and Ben had spent the afternoon unloading the last of the corn harvested on Gantry Champion and Sons' land that year. Ben, the youngest of the Sons and the only one who still remained on the farm, had sprawled for some time that afternoon in the truck-box on freshly gleaned, sun-warmed corn, sifting the kernels through his fingers. And then Julian had returned for the last time. In two days, he'd be gone, and it would not be Julian who would return again, Ben was sure.

Julian spoke. "So they finally hung her."

"Yeah." They looked at the portrait.

At the far end of the bar, Jimmy Wordsworth began to sing. He was drunk. When he was drunk, he lost his ability to talk. The regulars of Meek's Bar liked to watch him strike up a conversation early in the evening with strangers, people who'd never been to the bar before. Then, as the hours wore on, he'd become very quiet for a time, while his new acquaintances continued to rattle on and on about this and that. All at once, he'd stare at them and sing some western song or other in a deep, sonorous voice. And he wouldn't quit. He'd sing the whole number, and at the end, he'd always laugh in the same deep voice as he sang, as though the laugh were part of the song. People didn't listen to the song — someone always went to play the juke-box, and Mona, who had the volume control hidden under the bar the way some places had burglar alarms, turned it up loud. And Jimmy Wordsworth would be gagged for the rest of the evening. His real name was Wurmnest. He did odd jobs around town, like clearing snow and mending porches, for widows and single ladies, "girls," he called them. But people said he did a lot more for those women than that. Some said his "odd jobs" knew no limits.

She's worn out, Pal, and got none left.
It's you who took it, gone and shook it
So it's broke
And all in pieces.
> *Jesus, where's another?*
'Nother one to squeeze and shake
Hope on, wish on, till she break.

Wordsworth's voice soared and quivered like a hot prairie wind over a wheat field.

Ben knew Julian hated it when Jimmy sang. Julian slid off his stool, and, with a handful of change, approached the juke-box winking blues and purples in the corner. Ben swivelled on his stool to watch Julian.

Packages of flowered wrapping
Shining in your eyes.
Lover, dreamer, pulling ribbons,
Thinking life is in disguise —
Shake it, break it, till it dies.

Julian's thighs bumped in time to the music against the front of the juke-box when the first song finally clicked in with the coin. Ben watched his friend hunched over the selection panel as he had done many times since they'd been old enough to come here.

Something was different now. He feared Julian's turning back to his seat, wearing his new future like a silky red cape about his shoulders. But Julian did turn — swish, ripple, a flare of iridescence. Jimmy was silent.

Ben and Julian ordered more beer, and when Mona had brought it and curled up again in her niche, Ben said, "She's real, you know."

"Who?"

"Her." Ben gestured with his bottle to the portrait. "She's a real person."

"Well, it's a photograph, isn't it? She'd be real, all right."

Ben was irritated. "No, I mean the guy who took the picture really knew her. The guy who brought the picture here. Mona told me. She isn't just a model."

Mona's eyes focussed on Ben and narrowed when she heard her name. But her attention wandered again and dissipated with the smoke from her cigarette. The beat from the juke-box filled the space in which Ben expected Julian to ask about the guy and the photograph. But when Julian took a sip of beer instead, he remembered that Julian didn't ask questions any more. It was as though he'd already left, and his being here was just a post-mortem muscle spasm, a last twitch of centre-less nerves.

Ben went on. "He was an engineer in Fiji. Came from around here. Mona can't remember his name, but he was an older guy, travelled around a lot. When he was in Fiji, he had to spend a lot of time out on all these little islands, but he had his own place somewhere out there, and he met this girl, a native — he figured, anyway. He fell in love with her — 'in love with her' — jeez. That's what Mona says." Mona gave Ben a withering look.

"The girl turned out to be a real feisty kind of broad. Had a lot of guys on her tail and knew how to handle 'em. But she liked the engineer, I guess, and he got a better house and whenever he was in town he'd stay with her. He knew she probably played around while he was gone, but he was so proud of having this genuine Fiji-an princess, he didn't care. They even had a kid."

There was a break between records on the juke-box.

Wordsworth's song knifed through Ben's story as though it had
been mulling around the tavern the whole time:

It's you who took it, gone and shook it
So's it's broke
And all in pieces — Jesus....

Another record came on and Mona turned up the volume.

"The kid was blond. Fair and blond. The engineer wasn't blond,
and neither for sure was the girl. But this engineer, he didn't make
too much of it, right away."

"It wasn't his," said Julian. "Obviously."

"Maybe. But there weren't any other blond guys around that he
knew of. Just dark-haired, dark-skinned Fiji-ans.

"One day, the engineer finds out that the girl isn't a native at all.
She's a California girl that lived in Fiji most of her life and stayed
there when her parents left. Well, this guy was so pissed off, he
takes the kid and leaves — and showed up here about a year ago."

Julian shrugged. The story was typical small-town gossip.

"That isn't all. Mona says he lived in a bunch of places since Fiji,
dragging this blond kid around, before he got here. And he came
in one night and told Mona the story. But Mona said he got so mad
and crazy when he told her the part about the girl not being a Fiji-
an princess."

"He broke his beer bottle on the edge of the bar," said Mona.
"Snapped the neck right off."

"Yeah," continued Ben. "And he kept saying how she'd tricked
him and everything, and when Mona asked him if she didn't want
the kid back, and what had happened to the princess, he just cried
and cried."

Julian asked, "Where does the picture come in?"

"I went to his motel room a few days later," said Mona, "to see
if I could help with the kid, but Winnie — you know my cousin,
Winnie deBeer? She works there. She was cleaning his room and
she said he'd checked out and left some stuff behind, including that
picture. So I told Winnie he was a friend of mine and I'd keep it for

him until he came back."

"We figure he killed her."

Julian snorted.

Mona said, "He acted like it. And how come she hasn't come looking for her kid? He just acted like it. And he's running like a jack-rabbit, isn't he? Running from the cops."

Julian got up and walked behind the bar and began to lift the picture off its hook. "Don't!" warned Ben. He stood, and reaching across the bar, grabbed Julian's arm. "Don't, Julie."

"What's the matter? I just want to see if there's a name on the back."

"I don't want to know."

For a time the bar was silent except for quiet drinking and the last drumbeats of the juke-box tune fading away. Ben felt the nameless engineer occupying the stool between them. Mona tidied up the ashtray and the empty glasses in front of Jimmy Wordsworth, who was looking down into his lap, his unshaven face shadowed under a navy-blue baseball cap. As Mona wiped the ashes and sticky rings of liquor off the varnished wood, Jimmy looked up at her, as if to order another drink. "Packages of flowered wrapping shining in your eyes," he sang, the words clear and strong despite his body being slack with whisky.

Julian leaned across the empty stool to nudge Ben with his elbow. Ben turned and saw again the red cape glistening on Julian. "Well? Haven't you got anything to tell me about that rabbit up there?"

The straight narrow lane left the town abruptly. It had always been more a leaving road than a coming one, but like many country roads, it skinnied down once it hit the escarpment and dwindled into a pasture trail. It was hard and smooth this time of year. Julian accelerated his half-ton once they'd passed the last street-light, and Ben, flattened down on the seat next to the door, kept his eyes up so he could catch the stars falling. The moon was thin and hanging low, as if it had fallen, too.

After a few miles, Julian shifted down and nestled into his seat, as he'd always done. He took the beer Ben handed him and said in the direction of his own half-open window, "That engineer wasn't much different from her, you know. What was he doing out on the ocean looking for flowered princesses, anyhow?"

By looking straight out of his window and shielding his face from the brightness of the accessory lights and the headlights, Ben could see the occasional firefly shimmering in the ditches. His nose was against the glass when he said, "You're going to goddam Africa."

"It's part of my job. And it's for humanitarian reasons."

"Your job! You're a farmer!" Ben turned and spat the word. Julian looked at him and Ben could see the whites of his eyes glinting in the darkness.

"No, *you're* a farmer, Champ. It was never for me."

Ben put his leather heel on the dash. "Oh, it was always for me. I belong on a pile of corn, I'm part of the load. *You* go to University and all of a sudden you're an 'agricultural advisor.' Big deal."

Julian sighed. He squeezed the brake pedal and the truck pulled over to the side of the road. He got out and walked to the rear of the truck. Ben swallowed his beer, then opened his window and threw the empty bottle out. Julian came back with two more bottles which they uncapped with the seat-belt buckles. He was about to put the truck into drive when Ben said, "No, Julie, let's not go yet. Let's just sit here a while. We won't do this again for a long time."

Julian switched off the ignition and the lights. "Okay, dear, but I don't feel like necking tonight. I have this nasty headache...." Ben laughed, relieved, and put his other foot up on the dashboard, knees apart, head back.

They'd parked near a dike that still had a trickle of water in it. Teenaged boys in their fathers' cars came here to take pot-shots at muskrats and mallards, or gophers on the ridge. Ben and Julian had often come here, armed with twenty-two's and cokes, and sometimes with giggly young girls in shorts and white sandals and fruit-flavoured lipstick, girls who grieved in childish voices over the gophers the boys killed. In the daytime, herons flew out of the marshy dike-bottom when disturbed; at night, owls, silent and sure.

"What the hell you gonna do in Africa to pass the time?"

"Study alchemy, Champ. I found a great book on ancient chemistry in Toronto last week. It's about this thick, so it should keep me busy for a while."

"You always liked that stuff in high school." The sour taste of discontent seeped like acid into his mouth, his words. The liquor wouldn't wash it away. Ben forced a laugh. "Maybe you can find out how to change sand into diamond chips or something, or wheat. That'd be more up your alley."

"Up *your* alley." Julian thumped the heel of his hand against the steering wheel. "I heard that a lot of the foreign workers up there have apartments or beach-houses in Malta."

"Malta? What's that?"

"On the Mediterranean. They spend all their leave up there."

"You could get yourself a woman!"

"Yeah. I could get myself a woman." Their eyes met, their faces lively now as they both thought of the engineer.

Ben looked away first. "I'd like to have a mistress in Malta. I'd like that."

"Last year you wanted a new four-wheel drive tractor. Got one, too."

"I'll try giving it a hug next Saturday night. Or maybe it'll ask me out for Sadie Hawkins." Ben's tone was colourless again, dry.

"You know," said Julian. He paused and leaned forward so his chin touched the top of the steering wheel. "Years ago scientists were always heating things and boiling and burning and mixing all kinds of junk, always trying to turn one thing into something else. And they were always looking for magic potions in tree sap and plant juices — you know. Well, they used to think that metals that were burned or melted could be restored by re-burning them with wheat. I mean, they thought wheat could revive anything." Julian laid his cheek on the steering wheel and looked at Ben. "It could resurrect life."

Ben squinted and worked his face muscles to fight back tears. Julian threw open the truck door. "Hey, Champ — this is where we came graduation night, remember?" And now, Julian seemed like a parody of his younger self. "We had a christening, remember? We jumped into the creek in our new suits, and I christened you Champion of Beet Hollow, and you christened me — uh — Julian Caesar, Conqueror of Fair Damsels in Undress." His voice was high-pitched. "Remember? Come on!" Ben could see Julian's white running shoes pounding the road.

Autumn-tough reeds at the bottom of the dike slapped against Ben's thighs, and the cat-tails burst in his face as he ran to the water. He couldn't see or hear Julian. Only the portrait in the bar, the girl, luring him on with tropical vapours and a scent of flowers, and those sullen eyes. Julian called in a simpering falsetto, "Over here, Princess." Then a splash. "Come on, Benny-boy! Time for another christening."

Ben stood frozen at the edge of the stream. He could see Julian now, prancing in the cold, shallow water, shrieking and chattering his teeth, and in between the shrieks Ben could hear slithering and rustling, like jungle creatures closing in. He took a step forward, but Julian splashed up to him and yanked his arm. Ben fell on his knees into the stream. "Julie...."

"I christen thee." Julian held onto Ben's jacket collar and scooped water on his head, into his face. Ben clutched Julian's shirt at the waist. He was cold. The gleam in the portrait's eyes was cold, and he started to shiver. "Julie...."

"I christen thee," Julian thundered, "FARMER! You are a *farmer*, Ben Champion, so *be* one. *Be* a farmer, for Christ's sake!"

"Julie!" Ben's voice broke. He grabbed another fistful of Julian's shirt with his other hand.

"And me? I don't want a woman in Malta, Ben," said Julian. He held onto Ben's shoulders and felt Ben's body shaking with sobs, though he made no sound. "I don't think I want a mistress." The creek was still now — not even a breeze hissing among the bullrushes as Julian shook Ben. "And I sure as hell don't want to be one, either."

Julian dropped Ben off at Meek's Bar to get his car. Ben was soaked and very cold, but he went into the bar. Jimmy was there, of course, but he didn't look up. Ben asked Mona to make him a coffee, then sat on a stool and watched the rabbit's head on the wall. The light from the beer-ad clocks shone in its glass eyes, and Ben wondered whether, in its moment of dying, the rabbit had had visions of living again as a fox or a man with a .302.

The air smelled of old smoke and fresh ammonia. Mona slathered the tables with disinfectant. Her body undulated with the motion of the big grey rag in her hand as it swam back and forth across each surface.

Jimmy Wordsworth sang into his lap, "...flowered wrapping ...in disguise...." Nobody heard. Most of the seats in the bar were empty, and the portrait stared at no one.

Dream of the Half-Man

The night of the heart attack, Lou dreamed again the half-man dream. Sometimes in the dream the jacked-up Bronco soared above the freeway like a Disney incarnation, saving the limbs of the man snagged under its chassis. But most times, when things were going badly for Lou, the Bronco did not fly.

When she was on the brink of puberty, she'd been told the story of the half-man by her great-aunt Laverne, who had moved to Minneapolis to marry an American Lutheran. Laverne and the Lutheran told many horror stories. It was as though Minneapolis was under the tyranny of a sleek wheeled beast that slaughtered citizens at random on their six-lane highways. But the half-man story had disturbed Lou more than any other, for there had been no death. At least, not right away, and when it came, it was at the wrong time.

One hot Minnesota night in July, a man was on his way home from a bar from which he'd been expelled for drunkenness. He was driving a new Bronco with a raised suspension and over-sized tires because he had forgotten he was no longer the hellion he'd been in his youth, riding rough terrain in a high-powered truck with a girl at his side. In truth, he was over fifty and had never taken the

Bronco out of the city. In a blurred fury, he tore along the freeways and up and down exit ramps and access roads that would eventually lead him home.

Just past one of the exits, at an intersection, he missed a red light and took the corner at full speed into the path of a motorcycle ridden by a young man and his sweetheart. The sweetheart was thrown to the curb, but the Honda and its driver were entangled in the undercarriage of the Bronco, unnoticed by the drunk. He accelerated and scorched along a segment of straight urban highway heading south. He did not hear the screams of the boy under the truck, or perhaps he thought the screams were inside his own head.

Miles later, he turned onto a gravelled street in the woodsy suburb where he lived. Here the Bronco began to fail. It finally stalled. The drunk was sweating now. He'd begun to feel that something was wrong. Horribly wrong. He abandoned the Bronco and lurched towards his house. He could hear the anguished moans of the half-dead motorcyclist under his truck, but it was too late, he hurried on. Whatever it was, it was too late.

Aunt Laverne's husband's nephew lived next door to the drunk. He was working in his garage, repairing his own car, when the Bronco stopped near his house. He saw his neighbour stumble by and heard the terrible cries. With a socket wrench in his hand, he approached the deserted Bronco. Even from a distance, he could see motorcycle wreckage under the front end of the truck. He ran back to his own house and called an ambulance and a tow truck. The tow truck winched up the Bronco, and a rescue team dislodged the motorcycle and then the mangled half-body.

In a moment of clear thought, the boy said, "I'll kill him."

The story had rested there for many months. Lou often thought about the poetic half-man, without his right arm and leg, appearing in the drunk's doorway. She thought about the drunk man's nightmare of waiting for the half-man to appear with some indescribable weapon, indescribable hatred.

But then Laverne said that the drunk had died of a stroke before the half-man was mobile enough to get his revenge. That was when

Lou's dream began. In her dreams, she tried to save the boy on the motorcycle, and she tried to kill the drunk. Over and over again. In many different ways.

Last night, Lou's father began to pace and rub the lower part of his left arm, and he began to sweat and mumble. "Open the window," he'd said. But it was ninety degrees outside and no one did. "I'm coming down with something," he said to his wife, Audrey. *I'm coming down with something.* He lay down on the living room sofa and had his heart attack. Audrey called the hospital and the paramedics came and took him away.

Lou had come to her parents' house last night to tell them she was leaving the apartment she'd been sharing with her girlfriend and was moving back home for a while. She'd nursed her roommate through anorexia by convincing her that yogurt wasn't really food, that it had been pre-digested by a pugnacious species of bacteria, and now the roommate had found a boyfriend, and the two of them were edging Lou out of the three-room suite on Osborne Street. But Lou hadn't had a chance to tell her parents before the heart attack. Her mother followed the ambulance to the hospital. "Stay here, Lou," she'd said before she went. "I want someone to be in our house." Lou had gone to sleep in her old room so that her mother would not be alone during the night. Now she simply needed to collect her belongings from Osborne Street. She was home.

Awakening from the half-man dream, and the sounds of screeching metal, Lou heard scraping and clunking from the kitchen. She got out of bed right away and shuffled in old pyjamas to the kitchen. Her mother was on her hands and knees in front of the cupboard beneath the sink. She was surrounded by rusted tins of wax, and jars and bottles of cleaners and window sprays and drain openers. "I thought I heard a mouse," she said.

She needs to kill something, thought Lou. "Did you call the hospital?"

"He's stable."

Stable. The Bronco came to Lou's mind. "It's all that

cheesecake. Must've clogged his arteries. You shouldn't have made him eat it."

"You won't find a villain here to bash." Audrey was scattering mothballs in the dark cupboard. Her voice was hollow and bounced with a muffled ping off the metal pipes leading out of the sink. "Anyway, it's you, you know. He thinks Clint is on drugs. He thinks Clint will harm you some day."

On their first date, Clint had taken Lou to see his favourite movie, *The Attack of the Killer Tomatoes*. Then they'd gone to the A & W and he'd asked her to marry him by placing a tiny french-fried onion ring on her finger. Lou loved the little rings from the centre of the onion, so she accepted, and ate it. She told her parents about the movie and the mock engagement. They were uncomfortable. Then one day he came to their house with fresh lobster. He pulled the claws and tails out of a cooler of ice and told Lou's parents that they were a gift from a friend in neurobiology. Clint was wearing oversized overalls with nothing underneath and he had a cold. Lou's father thought he was a dopehead. Lou moved out of the house.

Now Lou said to her mother, "You just said there were no villains."

Audrey put all the tins and jars and bottles back in their places. "None and many." She stood up. Her face was blotchy and her breathing quick and shallow, as though she had worked hard. The braid she wore for sleeping sat on her shoulder like a bristled chameleon. Perhaps she hadn't slept at all.

They talked about breakfast, about the danishes and muffins in the fridge, about eggs. "Too much cholesterol," Lou warned. They finally agreed on toast and grapefruit, but eyed the butter with distrust and used fruit jelly instead.

"We'll go to the hospital right after lunch. Your grandmother's coming. She should be here by noon."

Lou's mother's mother: a cowardly, frail woman who'd had a heart attack once herself. Lou was about to make an unkind comment, but she felt sorry for the cheesecake remark, and answered, "Oh."

"Just what do you mean by that?"

"Nothing. If you want her here, good."

"She'll feel better."

"Should we clean the house or mess it up? What would make her happy?"

Audrey began to laugh. "She's been itching to get at the tiles in your father's shower. Between them, with Q-tips. But he would never let her. Finally she'll have her chance."

Lou laughed too, but Audrey was crying now, though she still made laughing noises and her mouth was compressed in a wide, close-lipped smile. Her breasts and shoulders trembled. Lou reached for her hand among the toast scrapings. "I hardly ever see Clint any more. And we were just friends anyway. We were never going together."

"Let's leave the dishes," said Audrey. "It'll give Mother something to do besides weep and nag when she gets here."

"Yes, let's not even clear them off the table."

A square of light shone on the white rug in the living room. The day would be hot and still, sedated, again.

His magazines were scattered on the coffee table where he'd sat down after supper — *Harper's* folded over at an article about terrorists, *Saturday Night* unopened, a pregnant vertical bulge along its stapled spine. Two cigarette butts lay in an ashtray beside the remote control for the TV, and next to that a package of Rothman's and a roll of antacid tablets. Packages: the magazines, the television, the cigarettes, the Rolaids. With them Lou's father managed his life, their lives, from the couch in front of the picture window. Whenever Lou came up the driveway, she saw his head above the back of the sofa, framed in the window.

Now she tried to remember her father in some other circumstance, tried to recall some moment of joy they'd shared. The only image that came to her mind was the time he'd found a stray female cat and new-born litter in the garage, had come into the house holding a tiny black kitten on the flat palm of his hand. Lou had been a little girl. Her father had laughed and laughed at the smallness of the kitten whimpering and mewing with its short claws hooked into his palm. Lou had wanted to keep the kitten in the house. But her father had taken it back to its nest behind the garbage cans and the next day the litter and mother were gone. "She moved them to a safer place," he had told her. He hated pets.

Lou sat down on the sofa and looked at the coffee table. She sat there a long time, not touching anything. She did not want to see her father in the hospital. She was afraid.

At exactly twelve o'clock, Lou's grandmother, Winnifred, arrived in a taxi, with greasy cabbage borsch and a suitcase and an umbrella. Lou watched her come up the front sidewalk, clutching the wrinkled paper bag to her chest, her glasses around her neck on a black cord. "Borsch and it's ninety," Lou said to herself. She recognized the two-litre shape of the mayonnaise jar outlined by the brown paper.

Winnifred's eyes filled with tears as soon as she had installed the soup in a forward position in the refrigerator, in front of the milk and beer. "Oh my dears," she said as she gave them each a feeble hug. "It's that filthy smoking. Maybe now he'll quit. Well, he'll have to quit. They'll make him. Louise, is your friend still vomiting up her food?"

"Every day," Lou lied. "Hello, Grandma Winnie."

"It smells of mothballs in here. I already have a migraine."

"Mother's trying to kill a mouse. All she'll do is chase it to another part of the house, and then she'll have to put out more mothballs, and pretty soon the whole house will be filled with mothballs and we'll all have to move out."

"I hate rodents."

"But at least there won't be any mice."

"You really should trap it, dear."

"Yes, we'll have to kill it," said Lou.

"Didn't you even wait for me to have lunch?" Winnifred asked, her eyes filling again.

Lou put her arm around her grandmother's waist. "Oh, those are still the breakfast dishes."

"You poor dears...."

"I see you brought your suitcase," said Audrey, lifting it to see how heavy it was.

"Yes, I thought I'd stay a few days. Should we have the soup now?"

"It's supposed to be cooler tomorrow."

"You should have closed your blinds hours ago."

Lou went back to the sofa and lay down. Her mother and her grandmother nipped at each other's ankles in the kitchen. The bickering lulled her into a half-sleep, and in her drowsiness she remembered the dream. It was just a flash, as memories of dreams often are — a face, the half-man being pulled with a hard, bright chain from under the Bronco. His face was her father's face.

When she awoke, her grandmother was walking through the living room with Mr. Clean and a box of Q-tips. "We're going as soon as your mother has had a nap." Her mother had never taken a nap in her life. "Oh Lou, you could at least have dumped the ashes. Here, I'll do it. And you can throw out the cigarettes — he won't need those any more. Here, give them to me."

Lou snatched up the Rothman's and took one out of the pack. She put the cigarette in her mouth and gazed loose-lipped and narrow-eyed at her grandmother. With chin a-quiver, Winnifred gathered up the magazines and the ashtray and the Rolaids, somehow making room for them between Q-tips and Mr. Clean, and minced into the hallway in her white Tender Tootsies.

I must set the trap before we leave, thought Lou. She kept the cigarette in her mouth, unlit.

There was a secret room under the basement stairway that had a small door on each side leading to two different rooms. It had been Lou's hideaway while she was growing up, and had provided a handy escape when her boy-cousins had chased her around the ping-pong room, bent on stealing kisses. Now it was the place where her father kept past fancies, like wine-making equipment and fondue pots. It was also where the mousetraps were stored. And it was cool.

The mousetraps were in a shoebox, with dried-up rolls of

Scotch tape, old screws, a meat thermometer that didn't work, wine corks, burnt-down candles, a broken pocket-watch, and a bottle-opener shaped like a woman's leg. There were other shoeboxes but the one with the leg-shaped bottle-opener was Lou's favourite. The contents of the box never changed. Nothing was ever added or taken away.

Lou took one of the traps out of the box and, by the glow of a dusty light bulb, read its inscription: *VICTOR, Woodstream Corporation, Lititz, Pennsylvania.* She took out the pocket-watch, too. What significance had it had in her father's life? She held it up to the dim light, looking for an inscription on its back, and ran her fingertips across the metal to feel what might have been engraved there once. It can't be important, she thought. He wouldn't leave it here in this box. But what did she know about her father's past, his souvenirs and his sadnesses? There was so little.

Lou sat down on an overturned laundry tub with the mousetrap in one hand and the watch in the other. The cigarette stuck to her lips and she made it flip up and down with gentle undulations of her lower jaw. Hollow rubbing sounds came from the shower stall off one of the upstairs bedrooms. Audrey must be back in the kitchen, now that it was safe. Lou thought about the dream. She'd never seen the half-man's face before. Her father retreated from her as each minute passed.

Then she heard another sound, a rhythmic gnawing, coming from behind her on the grimy shelves filled with empty pickle jars and ragbags and shoeboxes. A steady rhythmic grinding of small teeth on wood. Was he trying to get in or out? Lou said, "Hi." The gnawing stopped. He was in there with her. She looked at the mousetrap.

After moments of silence, the chewing began again. Lou pictured the mouse in the trap, tidy metal jaws clamped across the mouse's middle, cutting him in half, snapping his miniature spine.

A voice now, just above her, suddenly loud. "Lou? Are you down there? It's time to go."

The gnawing stopped. Lou was not ready to answer. The space she was in was quite small, but she had started to feel comfortable in it, for its dimensions had grown. She tossed the watch and the mousetrap into the shoebox. Nothing added or taken away.

"Lou?"

The naked doll with the harridan's hair and one arm missing stared glassy-eyed at Lou from the top shelf against the wall. The hand it had was raised above its head, fingers spread. The doll was propped up in a tobacco tin, from the days when Lou's father had smoked a pipe. It was the only doll Lou remembered having. She'd played mostly with toy six-shooters when she was growing up. Dolls had scared her.

She took the nameless, wild-haired child down from the shelf. Its severed arm was in the tin, and showed futile signs of repair. "Susie," said Lou. "I'll call you Susie." But she put the doll back on the shelf. As she was leaving the secret room, she thought she heard a ticking, like a watch. Or was it the sound of little claws scratching on wood?

Lou met her mother on the stairs. Audrey's hair was on top of her head now, its grey-white-auburn strands tied in a bun in the centre. She'd spent time rubbing cream into her face, and the massaging had evened out her complexion. She smelled of Chanel, but was still in her dressing gown. "You're like your father. He often comes down here to get something from one of those old shoeboxes, and he stays for ages, and comes back up empty-handed." She looked down. "And here you are, empty-handed."

In the car on the way to the hospital, Lou's grandmother told the story of the old man who'd slipped on ice and broken his leg. "I heard it at bingo," she said. "He was an old retired RCMP officer, someone important. He was walking on a street near his house last winter and he fell and broke his leg. And no one driving by stopped to help him, not for a long, long time. I don't know how long. It was terribly cold. I guess people thought he was a derelict of some sort. By the time he was rescued, he was very sick, and a few weeks later he died of a clot in his lung. The family blamed the passers-by for his death, for not stopping to help. But what good does that do? They don't know who to sue."

The hospital was not far away. Its windows stared at them and at the sky above the trees lining the hot streets. Her father would not be watching through one of the windows today, but he might be some other day. How would he look?

"I wish you hadn't told me that just now, Mother," said Audrey. "I had just begun to feel some hope. I wish you hadn't told it."

He should have had a sign, thought Lou. I USED TO BE A MOUNTIE. I AM NOT JUST ANOTHER BUM. HELP ME. She thought about the drunk and the Bronco, the drunk roaring around town, catching sober people under his torture-machine, and about sober people driving by an old man lying on the street, assuming he was just a drunk.

There was construction at the hospital, a new wing. In front of the building, they could see a huge excavation with piers and gridwork. Lou saw the hospital tipping over, dying men tipping out of their chairs and beds and wafting in white muslin to the mass grave beneath their windows.

The three women walked through a long temporary corridor that had been built at the edge of the construction site to join the parking lot to a side entrance. It was a white tube that echoed and rattled with their walking. The people in the corridor were like March hares and lonely Alices trying to get back through the looking-glass.

Winnifred said, "You'll find your father a changed man, if he...."

How would he look? Lou was angry at her grandmother for upsetting Audrey, and did not speak as they made their way to the third floor. They passed a gift shop. What could she bring him? A stuffed cat grinned at her from a high glass shelf.

Waiting for the elevator, Lou said, "Grandma Winnie, did Laverne ever tell you about the motorcycle driver that got stuck under this guy's truck?" She would tell her all the gory details. "And had half his body ripped off on the gravel, at eighty miles an hour?"

Audrey said softly, "My god." She walked away.

But Lou's grandmother was unflustered. "Yes, I remember that. Wasn't it just dreadful? Laverne's husband knew the driver of the truck, you know. His name was Teddy. But you're mistaken about the boy's injuries, dear. I remember his picture in a Minneapolis newspaper when I visited Laverne one Christmas. He was suing Teddy's estate for a ridiculous amount of money, considering he lost only an ear and part of his foot. After all, he can walk almost normally."

The elevator door opened. Audrey hurried to it and got on. As they rode up, she stared straight ahead, cold and angry. Winnifred looked at the floor, a pink Kleenex clutched to her throat. Lou felt tears coming and swallowed many times to get rid of them. "You could have tried to make me laugh," said Audrey, and slapped first Lou's, then Winnifred's buttocks with her handbag.

The elevator stopped at the third floor. "It's through that door," said Lou's mother, and they moved towards it.

My father is behind that door. I'll ask him about the watch.

They pushed open the door. Lou was less afraid now, only half afraid. Here I am, empty-handed. What do you bring a father? What if they only let us in one at a time? Perhaps he'll speak first. He'll say something like, "Who let you in?" Or, "Did you bring me a cigarette?" Or, "It must be a hundred degrees in this place."

Only an ear and part of his foot.

What had become of the half-man? Where was the horrible gun, held in the only hand he had left?

What will I dream?

"Did you set the trap, dear?" whispered Winnifred.

"Yes," Lou lied.

A Stone Watermelon

Cecil Miles nursed the blue and white Maverick over the first stretch of washboard road, the one they had to cross before Norman, who always poured, could safely uncap the rye bottle and pass around cups of warm liquor to the other three. They urged him to get the job done, what with the second stretch of washboard looming ahead. They didn't always go out by this road, but every surface had its various traffic scars close to town, and of course Norman couldn't pour while still in town, because of Henry Tufts — he had a blue-and-white of a sterner nature.

"Paper again?" asked Tully, sitting dour in the back seat beside Norman. "They always fall apart halfway through."

"Mine doesn't," said Cecil cheerfully from up front.

"Well, I got wetter hands." They always argued about the cups. Eddie Barnesky, Cecil's front-seat companion, had once cut his lip rather badly on a plastic rim, and had had to endure the unpleasantness of explaining to his wife when he got home. Cecil complained that styrofoam reminded him of hot coffee, and was all right for winter, but not a warm harvest day in August. Norman was in charge of supplies. It didn't seem fair to Arch Tully that Norman had purchased paper cups twice in a row.

Cecil fondled the Maverick's steering wheel with the palms of his slender hands, fingers splayed as though caressing a woman's ankle. "Old men aren't supposed to have wet hands, Tull," he said.

" 'At's the truth," said Barnesky in a voice that always reminded Tully of burnt toast. "We start to turn back to dust 'fore we even hit the grave."

The cups settled now — nestled on knees, between thighs, on leatherette arm-rests, on the dusty dashboard, steadied by aged hands and ritual — Cecil turned onto a road of fine, hard dirt and drove faster, though still too slowly to be mistaken for a man going about business. This was the summer ride, one of many taken in the warm green months of the year, and one much like all the summer rides taken together by the four country men in past years. August was one of the better times of summer, though, for seeing. The windshield blossomed with images of harvest-time — lifesaver-coloured threshing machines; vapours of fine straw that gleamed unexpectedly like minute fibres of brass behind the combines; heavy trucks trundling their loads over ruts in the fields; a flash of jack-rabbit leaping from some brief, perilous sanctuary; a bright human figure lurching among the machinery. The men in the car knew every change in the vista. In their part of the world, the roads were straight and orderly, and provided a faultless reference grid.

The passengers in the old nautilus had all retired, in one way or another, from the occupations of their more vigorous years. Cecil and Eddie had been farmers for most of their lives. Cecil had sold his land "lock, stock, and hen manure" to a businessman in Germany, well before such a practice was restricted by strident new laws. Eddie Barnesky had gone bankrupt "without the help of the friggin' big boys in Ottawa." Norman Tweed knew the countryside and the folks better than all of them because he'd sold thick vanilla in large bottles, and sweet lavender soap and furniture polish door-to-door, farm-to-farm, for long years, collecting, like the dust on his shoes, the history of his territory. Now the lives of the four men had become a review of the old methods, the old machines, the old society, and a commentary on the new, the changing times, the young generation pressing the land and each other too hard.

"Son-in-law brought me a stone watermelon slice from Mexico," said Tully, to get the conversation going, though he was seldom the one who initiated talk.

"Petrified," mumbled Barnesky.

"Seeds were painted on, I know that for sure," said Tully, ignoring Barnesky, as usual. "The rest was real green and real red. That's how onyx is." He squeezed his paper cup. "I was in Mexico once."

"You know," began Cecil, and his hands slipped around the steering wheel, "I grew watermelon for market one year. I can hardly remember it because I didn't keep much of a diary of the whole affair, just some notes in a dirty little memo book somewhere in a paper box. But I'm glad you mentioned that petrified watermelon, Tull — it reminds me of it quite well. I tried it again the next year, planting watermelons. They all froze. The young plants. In spring." He sighed, but still with the ever-present smile on his lips that he was known by in those parts. Not that he wasn't an emotional man. He never hid tears, even when he smiled.

"How'd you like Mexico, Tull?" came Norman's low, gentle voice. He tended to do that, to nurture Tully, where the other two didn't listen quite as carefully. Tully had lost a wife, a companion, and Norman Tweed had lost a friend who used to sit just where Arch Tully sat now.

Tully just peered through a corner of a side window, working the paper cup in his nervous hands. He was a late arriver in this fellowship — he never seemed to have quite caught the rhythms. He continued on the rides for the same reason as the others: he wanted to see again the Indian man pushing a woman in a wheelchair along a deserted road, miles from any farm settlement. Or something *like* that, something enigmatic rising from the line-straight horizon, a prairie mirage.

They'd seen the vision on a ride shortly after Arch had joined the group, in mid-summer. It was a day that had begun with one of those liquid mornings when everything flows with glycerine clarity.

That day's ride had started as a peaceful drifting. By afternoon, an odd but seemingly harmless weather system had developed in the broad sky — a series of brief squalls, very blue in the distance, with dramatic silver-edged clouds interspersed with the brightest sunlight, creating a play of shadows, of dark and light, on the prairie floor. Showers came and went. As the Maverick moved rook-like along the road-grid a few miles east of town, it passed in and out of the rain and sun, blues and greys.

They had just turned onto a particularly barren road, a narrow, smooth clay road, when they saw, very far off, a moving figure and a flash of white metal. Shifting winds tossed the grasses and the young trees that grew in the ditches, dappling the motions of the figure. Cecil slowed the car and the men watched the mirage come towards them, pass through the shadows of the clouds. It took a long time.

A dark-skinned man pushed a wheelchair, a man with a scarred, angular face. He looked old, veins of white ran through his hair. She was in the wheelchair, a strong-looking Indian woman who would have been tall had she been able to stand. She held a swatch of long, ebony hair over her face with a brown hand, a demure gesture revealing one glittering eye. Neither of the two travellers was dressed for showers or the cool of a sunless dusk. All around them hung silken wisps of rain. There was no discernible destination on that vast ocean for such a fragile vessel.

No answer for it. The men watched through the back window for a long time. Then Cecil launched into a disjointed account of an Indian who'd been his hired hand on the farm many years ago. Norman said softly over and over, "Where could they possibly be going?" Eddie Barnesky rubbed his eyeglasses on the sleeve of his plaid shirt and said, "'At's weird! 'At's weeeird!" Tully said nothing. He pressed his forehead against the side window. There was no answer. The Indian strode onward as though propelled by the strength of the woman in the chair.

And so the summer ride often came back to the narrow smooth clay road, where the four men in the blue and white Maverick searched privately for some remnant of a mirage which each felt belonged solely to him.

Norman probed, "Go there with your family, Tull?"

"Get the shits?" called Eddie from the front in his thin, constipated voice. Tully's lips tightened. He wanted to tell them about the woman with the camera in the terraced restaurant on the cliff, who'd come around to take pictures of the patrons, the lighted rocks, and the ocean behind them. About the picture, and how it stood for two decades on the piano in the sitting-room, and then disappeared on the day of his wife's funeral, as though she'd spirited it into the grave with her. But he couldn't get a story like that out, couldn't cover up the edge of it the way the others could.

They reached an intersection of farm lots, dark green with the rapunzel-glow of stubble beyond. "My old place," Cecil sighed and gestured with a flat hand towards one of the neatly-trimmed yards. "I was raised in a wee shed of a house right on that spot there. Lived of course in that bigger home later, near by, but when I was still a kid I always went back to that shack because I remembered something I'd left there. It was an old box camera — wasn't really mine, I don't think — just a cousin's forgotten — but I knew it'd been left there, even thought I knew the particular cupboard, a high-up one in the kitchen. I'd never taken a picture with it. I was terribly young, and I just adopted that camera in my mind. But after we moved to the bigger house, I went back often to look in that cupboard. It was never there. And the shack got crumblier and smaller as I grew, but I always thought about that camera. When they tore the place down, I examined the ruins and talked to the fellows, in case they'd come across it."

Assorted grunts from the others in the car. Tully thought, And where could that photograph have gone?

"Same thing with a B.B. gun I lost," said Barnesky. "Never found it, neither. Had to use a stick for a gun. Poked my sister with it in the eye."

Norman poured another round while meadowlarks warbled through the open car windows. When Tully shivered, though it was warm, Norman steadied the bottom of the cup, just below Tully's fingers, and sloshed a bit of whisky into it. The Maverick puttered on and on, sometimes shrouded in threshing dust, sometimes flanked by clean horizons. Cecil turned up the radio a little and Norman sang along with a woman who was crooning old tunes in a broad-sky prairie voice.

> *So you take the high road*
> *And I'll take the low,*
> *It's time that we parted,*
> *It's much better so.*
> *But kiss me as you go...*

sang Norman. He did not falter on the word *kiss*, thought Tully.

And then they were at Eddie Barnesky's old farm, and it occurred to each that perhaps Cecil was planning to visit all their ancient ruins, methodically, one after the other, unlike previous times when coming upon a familiar place unexpectedly by way of an indirect route bewildered them.

Eddie's home had burned down mysteriously before the new owners could settle into the square house with the sagging porch that went around three sides. All was white and bungalow in the yard now, but the image in the Maverick's windshield was of rough, charred foundation surrounded by a wintry landscape. And a memory of Eddie, staring dry-eyed out of the car window at the wisps of ash churned up by the incantations of a north-west wind.

"Folks all have orange jackets that glow like highway signs. Kids, everything. Piled out of their Datsun wearing those glowing jackets like they were exploring the moon or something. Said they were gonna have horses. Shit! Fella's thighs rubbed together when he walked."

Tully remembered the family well. Soon after they'd built a new house on Barnesky's old place, the Maverick — new then — had happened upon the alien tribe stranded on a road a few miles from their home. Their yellow Datsun was at the side of the road with its hood up, and all five of them sat around it as though they'd just bagged a prize buffalo. "What's on their heads?" Tully had asked, for every member of the family was wearing tiny head-phones, and, of course, their Day-glo jackets. "Walk-men," swaggered Cecil Miles. "Shit," mumbled Barnesky.

The parents and children had all stood up as the Maverick passed, but none removed their headphones, so Barnesky told Cecil not to stop but to continue on, and then stared dry-eyed at them through his window, just as he was doing now. "Well, I see Nora's clothes-line's gone the way of the garter belt," he said. "I expect they've got a microwave oven and scented toilet paper, too. Speaking of which, when we were dealing, I one time got a letter from 'em on fancy paper that had *all* their names pizzazzed across the top and some cartoony little crest or something in the corner." Eddie stuck a thumb-nail between his teeth. "Put it in the outhouse 'mongst the Sears catalogues." He sucked a tooth. "Wonder if they've got to it yet."

Then the shouting began inside Tully, as it did every ride about this time, when the colours of the air and Barnesky's ponderous commentary and Norman's steadiness and the endless, endless forward motion of the crowded little car all vibrated together. He wanted to slow it all down. He shouted inside at the vibrating, unchanging rhythms.

They got onto a smooth road again, a smooth clay road that murmured softly beneath the wheels.

"...Arch....Arch....Tull!" There was Norman, whispering at his ear, pulling with a tailored hand at Tully's khaki sleeve. Norman's lips puffed out in a sort of pout, which was the way he smiled, and the smile was saying, "You won't like this, but play along." Out loud, Norman said, "Your place," and he pointed with his chin past Tully's shoulder. Before he looked out, Tully looked down at his own hand, and saw it clenched around the paper cup, so tight that the cup had buckled at the sides and the whisky in it was quicksilver shouting for escape. Tully wanted to throw the cup at the back of Cecil's head, but there wasn't enough distance in the tiny car to make any more than a feeble pop, a futile pop with a paper cup, a useless rage. So he hung on to it, though Norman was pouring a fresh one for him.

Cecil said, "Archie, your front door is loose. I hope it wasn't vandalism." No, the door had always been loose. "It won't sell well, Archie, if you don't paint it and fix the door, and maybe burn down that old smoke-house back there, and maybe that tool-shed, too." Don't want to sell it, they got the land. "Or are you planning to move back here yourself?" Cecil eyed Tully in the rear-view mirror. Tully stared at the folded paper cup and tried to subdue the shouting by crimping the rim of the cup with his thumb.

"God, let's piss," mumbled Eddie.

Why here?

Cecil's splayed hands slid around the steering wheel, and they turned into the driveway of Arch Tully's yard. The junction with the road was marked by two upright angle-irons that each had, at its zenith, a red reflecting eye to make the driveway easy to find in the dark. She had always begun singing when, coming home after dark in winter, she saw the red eyes looking at her through the night snow.

Cecil was saying, "...check for vandalism. I'm surprised the windows are still unshattered." They never stopped at the old places. Tully noticed a cloud of threshing dust rising above the shelterbelt at the back of the yard, and all at once the noise of machines ground through the warm still air.

They stopped. Three of the men disappeared behind the grey one-and-a-half-storey house, but Arch Tully slouched near a roll of toothless snow-fencing in the front yard and stared through the weathered walls of the cottage. Beyond it, the dust veiled the blue intensity of the sky. The too-bright colours and sounds pierced the thin covering of his memory, and he shuffled towards the front porch for shelter, to have the sagging roof hide the sun and mute the gnashing of the combine's teeth. A creeping vine grew happily among the framework of the porch, but the philodendron in the clay pot beside the door had long withered, though it still clung to a stake in the hard soil. Setting the plant out had been Arch's final act when he moved out of the house two years earlier. It had been a simple act of frustration — he hadn't known what to do with the plant, it hadn't occurred to him to take it to his new apartment. So he'd set it out like a cat, hoping it might fend for itself. But he knew now it hadn't had a chance, probably knew it then. He just hadn't wanted it to die in the house.

And then, though there was no wind, Arch could hear the slatting of her flannel sheets on the wash-line near the garden. He retreated into the house.

The stove was still in the kitchen. He'd wondered if the stove would be there. He had once explored an abandoned house where there'd been a huge hole in the kitchen floor. The stove was hunched down in the cellar below. The kitchen floor had slowly rotted away. Arch always wished he'd been there when it happened.

But this here-and-now kitchen, with its calendar marked full of doctor's appointments, and the chiffon curtains with fallen dust layered in their folds, and the wall clock unplugged at 12:06, did not provide the protection Arch Tully sought. There was nothing for it but to continue. He walked, straighter now, into the barren hallway beyond the kitchen, the smooth, narrow hallway, and into the sitting-room whose windows faced north. The piano was still there, magnificent in the emptiness of that room, poised in a silent strength that held on to the melodies she had struck on its sounding board.

She was in the room. Arch picked up the photograph with both hands and heard the familiar rasping of the glass loose in the frame. He carried it to the window and wiped the glass clean with the pale edge of her brocade drapery. She stood in front of the smoke-house near a blossoming crab. The wind nudged a thick lock of hair across one eye, making her look coy, even raffish, instead of middle-aged and impatient with a husband who had called her away from hanging wash to pose for a picture in front of white blossoms. Reluctance hung about her like the faded apron she wore.

Arch looked through the window into the yard. The others were examining the decaying smoke-house, pushing on the wood with the flat of their hands, swinging the door open and shut, kicking the rot at the bottom. They began to move back towards the house, and each in turn passed the window and saw Tully standing there with the photograph in one hand and the drapery clenched in the other.

Perhaps there'd been no picture of the two of them in the terraced restaurant. He'd seen the senorita with the camera. He was sure he'd seen other couples posing for glossy photos. And he remembered wanting to be daring enough to ask the senorita to come to their table. But perhaps he never had, because at that time already, twenty years ago, the exultation and rapture of their union had long been replaced with weariness of changeless living. And it was well before the Mexico trip that she had begun to look at him as though she were seeing him through a telescope held the wrong way around. Still, he'd kept on believing that the glossy photograph had been on the piano every evening when she played. It wasn't here now. Cecil and Barnesky were probably confused — there'd never been a box camera or a B.B. gun, either. They were dreams.

Arch felt something tickle his cheek and wiped it away with the brocade still in his hand, leaving a shadow of dust on his pale skin. He heard Cecil and Eddie and Norman come into the room. They all commented on the piano. Norman blew on the ivories and slapped them with his white handkerchief, and sat down to play.

Arch turned and placed the picture back on the piano. "Anyway, it's not here," he murmured.

"What's that, Tull?"

He didn't answer. Norman continued to improvise on the piano keys, something slow and blue. Cecil smoked by the window. Eddie Barnesky shuffled about the room and ran stubby fingertips along cracks in the plaster. The shouting inside Tully was fading, whispering now of rest and sleep on a sofa in front of a window where the sun warmed the cushions.

A loud throat-clearing from the sitting-room door jolted the four men. Cecil and Norman and Eddie Barnesky and Arch Tully turned and saw a stranger there, although not a stranger, because he was easily recognizable as a thresher, and such a man was not a stranger to farmers and travelling salesmen. His hair was flecked with bits of straw, and grease stained his jeans and shirt-sleeves. He was young, embarrassed, dry of mouth. Finally, "We're short a vehicle. Uh—you guys goin' back to town? Soon?" His tone was half-hearted—he'd seen the Maverick in the yard, but hadn't expected to see four old men in the sitting-room of an abandoned house.

As they passed through the kitchen, Tully grunted, "Stove's still here."

The blue and white Maverick moved towards town. "Joy-ridin', are ya?" the young man had asked as they'd squeezed into the car and he'd seen the bottle and the cups. He sat thin between Cecil and Eddie in the front seat.

"Did you smell that sweat!" Eddie said when they'd dropped off the stranger.

At the corner in town where they always met and disbanded, they began the ritual of separation. Cecil brushed bits of luminous straw from the seat, not onto the floor but into his open hand. Eddie gathered everyone's cups and the extras and the strays. Norman blew into the unused cups and stacked them. His soft hands made comfortable rustling sounds. And Tully, on silver wheels among dappled blues and frosted clouds and tossing grasses, glided over the horizon along a smooth clay road.

The Edge of the Cornfield

"Don't hang up." The words are quick and breathless, spoken even before the receiver is at my ear. "Don't hang up. Please." But I do hang up, without saying hello. Not angrily, not with that sharp crack of smooth, hard plastic on steel, but gently and—almost—regretfully. I must hang up, because of what you said the first time you called. A stranger, and yet your words make me afraid you are someone who knew me once. But it is impossible.

It is the fourth call. They're never at the same time of day, or of the week, and sometimes the voice sounds far away, as though he is calling from underneath the sea, which is far from here. The voice, no matter how distant, fondles and cloys, even in such few words as he is able to say before I cradle the telephone receiver, "...don't hang up...."

They told me not to come here, to these two old rooms in this old building that smells of fish and camphor all the time, and smells of fish and camphor here, now, though I am sprinkling leaves of rosemary into the sauce bubbling on the stove.

The hallways are painted the colour of a tropical ocean after a hot, oily rain, and it is this heavy, oriental sea-colour that seems to exude the smells of fish and camphor. The fluorescent glare of my windowless kitchen tries to burn away the alien sounds and odours and textures of this old ruin so far from my clean, green fields. On these streets, in these two rooms, I ache with time passing, and my phantom lover's calls knell the hours like a tower clock. Look at my fingers, gone white and wrinkled like the corner-store cabbage. The dull edge of the knife is the dullness of my own mind.

I used to eat my meals by the window in the other room, the window where neon beer signs across the way turned the red of my wine from titian to indigo to scarlet, over and over, flavouring my simple food with colour, making rich the sun-starved fruits of plastic gardens. And through the windows I'd watch the people under the beer signs, people who were smudges on the dirty pane, and by the way the smudges moved I was able to decipher their moods. And when it rained and streaks of clean glass allowed me to peek at their faces, there was no one there to see, because it was raining.

But now I must stay away from windows. I will dine at the kitchen cupboard, facing a photograph of an old woman who warned me not to go. She does not call me. My mother has brushed me away without a thought, like cobwebs out of corners in spring.

There is French jazz on the radio, azure tones that permeate my skin and play my nerves like harp strings. I turn out the lights in the two rooms, and when I go to my bed, I nearly forget to check the lock on the door, the old door with the old-fashioned skeleton key, a fitting key. How many other keys like it drift from one man's hand to another in the city outside?

Just before I fall asleep, I remember the way my collie, after years of tender nipping and pouncing, finally with no warning clamped his jaws on the back of my tortoiseshell cat, his lifelong companion.

Is the caller someone I know?

The buzz of my alarm clock is not like a telephone bell, yet half in sleep, I spring out of bed and blunder with sand-filled eyes towards the kitchen wall. I pull the receiver to my mouth, I shout, "Hello? Hello?" It takes several seconds before I know no one is there. I stand several seconds longer with the earpiece pressed to my cheek while voices from outside and from the corridor filter through my sleep and my dream, and it comes to me that it is morning. Shouts of play-bound children and angry mistresses jab at me through the keyhole of the apartment door.

The dusty sitting-room window lets in some light, and I dare to stand by it for a moment. Certain shadows and reflections I've come to know tell me there is sun this morning. I will not need my umbrella today.

While the old woman watches me pick through a shabby jar of olives to find just one more that still has its jewel-like centre, a telephone rings. I concentrate on my searching, and try to imagine it is the phone in the next apartment. But the ringing is coming from my telephone. He's never called in the morning. It could be — someone else.

He says my name. This time I drop the receiver into the cradle. It is a shard of ice that numbs my fingers. He knows my name. He knows who I am.

I *must* go to work. I must go to work to keep my daily appointment with the skew-mouthed, firm-fleshed boy who buys sweet, raw Brazil nuts from my uncle's stall every morning at eleven when he finishes jogging across the Mid-town Bridge and back again. I've seen him only when his hair is sticky and limp, his face wet from exertion. But I watch him buy his paper cup of honeydew from the stand across the promenade, and then he comes to my stall — my uncle's — and I look at his eyelashes, which are longer than any I've seen on the few men I've really looked at up close.

He does not look at my face.

I pour the olive dregs down the toilet, and put on my Mary Quant hat, which might be a disguise, though Uncle would frown if he dropped in at the stall today. He has instructed me to wear white blouses and keep my hair pinned back from my face so that I will look "fresh and clean and crisp, like kohlrabi."

Half-way through the morning, it begins to rain. No one comes to buy. Some of the concessions close up. I keep my stall open, in case the boy comes, and stare at the honeydew stand across from me. Soon, a man wearing a suit and carrying a black umbrella that covers his face comes to buy pumpkin seeds, and while we listen to the dull plopping of the raindrops on the umbrella, the man gives me some coins. But they aren't enough, and when he gropes for the wallet in his back pocket, his jacket moves aside and I see something shining silver above his belt, like the handle of a gun. I take the bill too nervously from his soft hand, wishing I had taken the coins he'd offered first, and in my haste knock the bags of seeds to the wet ground. He picks them up, and as he walks away I see him wiping the muddy package against his sleeve, as though perhaps they are to be a gift for someone.

Still, I watch for the boy, and so compressed am I into that one expectation, I do not wonder at all that a faceless man carrying an umbrella and a gun would come to buy pumpkin seeds on a rainy morning.

I shutter the stall, finally, and walk in the direction of the bridge, past the cement park, past the relic steam engine that looks as if it's been still-framed in a vintage film, past the red-brick houses with the wrought-iron gates. A figure darts out from a side street, running, and I freeze. But it is only someone hurrying to get out of the rain.

And now, the streets seem to be full of people running. I hear the clatter of flat-bottomed running shoes on the drenched pavement all around me. One of them will be him, on his way from the bridge to buy Brazil nuts. I picture him now, very wet, with his clothes and hair clinging so that he is sleek and thin and shimmering. But the clatter is merely the intensity of the rain, falling harder now in bigger, heavier drops.

I turn to go back, but as I glance at one of the brick houses, I see a figure of a man. He is in a second-storey window and he is watching me. A man in a suit is watching me through the downpour of grey. His hand moves, perhaps to wave to me, or to reach for something.

Beneath him, in front of the door, sits a cat, its fur flattened and dark, its ears drooped and bent to keep out the raindrops, and I can just make out a wretched lump of mouse at its feet.

The apartment building where I live is so quiet in the afternoon. Even the street outside is empty as I hurry, stiff with cold, from the bus stop a block away. Today, the corridor oozes its viscous colours and odours into the air around me, and as I twist my thin key in the lock, I think, for the first time in years, of cornfields.

When I was younger than ten, both in years and in living, I ran through cornfields unafraid, knowing that in any direction lay an edge of open space where I could get my bearings and find my way home. Mother was not always there when I arrived at the back door with my straight yellow bangs stuck to my forehead. She made brief escapes often in those days, and I, safe in cornfields, believed in the necessity of her many excursions, usually to the city. I could not, then, have recognized her loneliness; I thought she complained too much, and that she knew too little of the outside world that was Father's and mine. It was this world, Father's and mine, that her bitter voice would infiltrate late at night while I lay in bed straining to hear Father's soft-spoken answers.

One autumn, while I was playing in sunshine, feeling warm and fine, Mother bought a fur coat. Not an expensive one, nor mink, and it was "slightly used," smelling faintly of moth-balls. But she had saved up the money for it, then mended it and "spiffed it up" at her sewing machine in the kitchen corner where she also kept her books. She could not sew very well. We admired the coat, with its dark, rich sheen, the aura of glamour with which it enveloped the plain woman in the kitchen.

As autumn harvest drew on into shorter and shorter days, days of chill, white skies, Mother slipped as undiscernibly and as surely as those days into her own kind of winter. One day after school I found her flitting about the house. When she saw me, she scolded about a ribbon I'd lost from one of my braids. Then she told me she was going out and wouldn't be home until late. She dressed up nice and wore her fur coat.

As Father and I worked in the grain bins that evening, it began to snow, huge, sloppy flakes that made a sizzling noise when they landed on the dusty, dry yard.

When I went back to the house alone, I found it the way I'd left it, except that a glow of light shone from Mother's sewing corner. The sewing machine cabinet was open, and Mother was slumped over on it, still wearing her coat. Her head rested on the soft fur of her sleeve, and one of her hands curled protectively around a glass of Father's whisky. There was nothing else on the cabinet — no bit of mending, no new ribbons for my braids. Her eyes were closed and she was very still, but I'd never seen Mother sleep and couldn't tell whether or not she was sleeping then. But it was the coat that surprised me most. The fur was wet and stuck down, almost matted, as though she'd stood for a very long time in the snowfall, perhaps right outside the bin where Father and I had hammered nails into fresh clean boards. The sheen on the coat was no longer glamorous, and the smell of camphor was strong in the room.

In my child's mind, I trusted Father to take care of this unusual circumstance; but in a deeper, older part of me, I learned on that day that my mother was not safe in cornfields, and in the autumn that followed, I played in them less and less.

I didn't see the coat again until the morning of my father's funeral, when I saw Mother go to her closet and briefly finger the hem of the sleeve. She never wore it again.

She watches me from the photograph, older than her years, older than she wanted to be, older than she thought she could ever become. She always came back in those early years, but now I've left her, and though I expect to see her again one day, she's already brushed me away, knowing that *she* never wanted to come back. Staring at her picture, I feel a slow-moving peril creeping towards me from a great distance, that great distance beneath the sea, and it occurs to me all at once that I have not taken a breath for a long time. The air is so heavy, and though I sit very quietly, and there is no other sound, I sense someone in the hall coming towards my door. At first, the sensation is not strong enough for me to react. But the wave finally touches shore and I turn to look at the door, at the doorknob, and at the keyhole, and again I remember that the door is not locked. I steal across the room and take my key from the top of the refrigerator, and just as I insert the key in the lock, I feel — I am sure — another key enter from the other side. And as I twist the key, the other key twists the opposite way. It wants to unlock an unlocked door. The metal strains behind the brass plate. I press my forehead to the door-frame and funnel my energy into the key. A key must break, mine or his. Then I feel the other withdraw, as if my opponent has had a change of heart. My key completes the turn and the bolt clicks conclusively in the latch.

At night I dream of a man in a suit pacing his room while staring at a large, emphatic telephone on the desk by his bed. He paces and paces and swears in an unearthly dialect that needs no translation, so expressive is it in its curious blends of sounds and rhythms. He paces and paces, and then, with cold precision rather than uncontrolled rage, he takes a silver-handled gun from his belt and shoots at the telephone many times. The bullets travel slowly from the gun to the telephone, and though they are large and the shots echo as in a vault, the telephone does not shatter, nor even crack or bend. My place in the dream is unclear, perhaps that of a voyeur.

In this morning of invisible sun, I emerge from sleep chanting ancient numbers like a long-lost charm retrieved from the bottom of a well. I press my fingertips to the telephone dial for a few moments before defining the code that will reach at last beyond these barriers towards the familiar, clean, green fields. And there, it is her voice, coming from far away. And I am not sure at first if she is really saying my name, here and now, or if it is simply another phantom seeking to violate me in some terrifying and intimate manner. But the third time she says my name, I hear the beginning of panic rising in her voice, and I know that I must speak, so that we may begin, finally, to make our way out of the cornfield, to find the edge, to find out if it is still there.

Monolith

"My, that fan snores! We haul it out, though, summer after summer, and put it on the same window sill—noisy thing!

"Only morning and it's hot. These tarts are out of the freezer. Have one. It's too hot to bake these days. I see you've been going through the albums. Well. I'm glad you're back, Girl, even if you aren't staying."

Butter tarts — wrinkled on the top like elephant skin. I love the sound the ice cubes make in the tea-pitcher, that cheap Co-op store pitcher. If I shake the table ever so slightly, they ring, in the same arpeggio they have rung all these years.

Father's taking the wood pole to the rye field to mark the big stone. He's always the same, too, blue cloth cap, red hanky. He seems short to me now, and his hands are so small. Funny I never noticed that when we played "Blueberry Hill" together on the piano.

"There goes your dad to mark the stone. Almost time to combine that rye. Sure sign when he heads off with the pole. Funny, he always knows where to find it, even when the crop's grown up all around it. He just...senses it.

"Look at the crooked air over Jansen's summerfallow. You think there are vapours in that air, coming up out of the dirt, but if you go there, it's just hot.

"He's worried because there's no rain. Late crops need it. My, it's good to have you sitting there again, someone to talk at."

Couldn't we just sit and drink tea?

"The year that you were three years old was the driest year we've had here. It's hot and dry today, but.... You don't know what the summer was like, even the winter before, and the spring. The spring! I remember one windy April day standing just there, in the middle of the yard, looking at the sky, because it was so gloomy out, and still there wasn't really any feeling of rain, and the grey in the air was not clouds or fog, and it was too early for forest fires out east. But there was just something dark and...and dead about the way the day looked. Oh, the snow'd been gone a long time, already in April. There'd been lots of warm, warm days by then. And that was queer, too.

"But on this day, you were throwing dry weeds over the fence into the pigpen — there — and I felt the wind really pick up. I looked west across Dad's fields and I saw this big cloud coming, sort of a greyish, rolling cloud. Like a cloud of grasshoppers. I thought for a while it was a squall of rain, and I listened and listened for thunder, looked for lightning, but it wasn't there, and the air was dry, dry.

"Do you remember it at all?

"I picked you up and held you and watched, feeling a bit scared, hoping not to scare you."

I don't remember the pigs. But I remember all the dead trees that were here years ago, when I was little. Old dead trees with smooth trunks, no bark. Father said the pigs killed the trees by rubbing against them with their pink skin. To me, then, pigs were delicate animals, the prey of wolves, innocent and naked. I didn't understand how the rough bark could become so torn and shredded by their pink flesh. I remember having dreams about piglets squealing in pain, their flesh torn and shredded, and bleeding into the dust around the smooth trunks of dead trees. Rough and tender.

When I came into the kitchen very late at night years ago, I looked into the next room where you and Father slept, and I saw Father sleeping with his hands on your shoulders. His hands always looked coarse, and felt coarse when he held mine on the sidewalk in town, and I wondered how they felt on your shoulder. I remember the goat we had that summer, when he milked it. I tried to be gentle with the goat, but she didn't like my hands. But Father's hands, even fresh from untangling a snag of barbed wire, his hands on the goat's teats soothed her. I could tell by the slow blinking of her eyelids.

"We stood there and watched till the cloud came. Only, it didn't ever really come, in any big way. It was all dust, you see, dry dust carried here from further west where the soil is lighter. And that was the horrible thing about it. I knew it was dust and dirt — I could taste it, and see it blurring out the trees on the creek-bank. But it didn't have any body to it, the way rain or snow does. That was the horrible thing. That dirt couldn't be replaced, like you replace a worn-out wool coat. I just felt such a helplessness at the idea of all that soil being swept across the prairie on a hot grey April day that should have been lovely and green and sweet-smelling, you know?

"Now you have an idea how dry it was. And later in summer, where the snow usually drifted up in winter — you know, up against Kruegers' fence and the machine shed and the tall grass and the poplars there — well, all along there in summer, you'd find drifts of black dirt. I thought it odd. Familiar though, something I'd seen in old pictures. It was odd and still, it was familiar, like Grandma's queer lace cap in the album."

Like my Sunday school class. The photograph of my Sunday school class wearing brown jumpers and white blouses, and the boys in pants that came just to the tops of their shoes so that you could see that their white socks were clean ones. Yesterday afternoon when I walked to the edge of the yard, I felt that the whole Sunday school class should be there with me, holding those little red hymnals in that lazy way that they always did, their wrists breaking every so often, as though the books were too heavy. They stood there next to me under the white July sun, singing with the grasshoppers...

> *This is my Father's world.*
> *And to my listening ears,*
> *All nature sings*
> *And round me rings*
> *The music of the spheres.*

...and the boys would always shout the one line in the chorus, "Of rocks and trees! of skies and seas...." Rocks and trees. I wanted to yell out these words, too, but the girls never did. And no one ever asked about "the music of the spheres." How many of them know now, I wonder.

Father going to the rye field to mark the big stone. I don't know why he hasn't removed the rock after all these years. He talks about moving it every fall after harvest, or blasting it. We used to joke about it when we sat on it to eat tomato sandwiches the day they combined the field that it's in, or when Mr. Krueger came for the last supper and the last autumn beer. But it's been there since the day he came. You never get after him to move the stone. You never talk about it, have never been with us when we've looked at it, or sat on it to eat the tomato sandwiches you made for us. You were always in the house, still are, I guess.

Yesterday when I was in the garden looking at the house, it looked so lonely, and with the heat-shimmers coming up from the black earth between me and the house, I thought the house, with you in it, would rise on those hot vapours and take you to Oz. But it's Father, perhaps, who visits Oz.

"That summer, when you were three, we went for lots of walks, mostly to the creek. One evening, at dusk, it was so calm we could hear the owl hooting way off at the creek. What a time it was!

Queer, though, as it had been all along. It was fairly cloudless, I remember, and you know that colour of sky at dusk, I don't know what colour you call it.

"Now, instead of mist coming up from the fields, that'd be normal for a summer evening, there was a low-lying settle of dust making everything gauzy-looking. You and I went to look for the owl.... Oh, we had Peach then — remember the collie, Peach? He came along.

"We walked to the creek and found the owl, or rather, just the shape of him in the willows, and we watched him till it was dark. Except that it never got dark, quite, at that time of year. Never quite dark. It irritated me, somehow, still does now, when the sunset sneaks across the northern horizon.

"It sounds nice doesn't it? Now? I've made it sound so. It was as nice as I said, I suppose. But *then*, you see, I hated it, hated the calmness of the evening and the hooting of the owl, and that sky-colour. And while we walked back, I'd stop once in a while and you and Peach would wander off, leaving me standing there, staring at the house, with that one little light over the kitchen sink shining through the dust all the way to where we were in the field, and I wondered and wondered how I could possibly make it all the way back...."

I know the names for the colour of that sky, all kinds of names. Beth and Margaret and I used to name colours and show off our adjectives when we were in seventh grade. We called that colour "sapphire" for the longest time. Beth said sap-fire the first time she read it out loud in a book. And then Margaret suggested it might be "azure." I think she got that from a Harlequin romance. But we decided azure was more green, a sea-colour perhaps. I found "lapis lazuli" in a poetry book in the school library and surprised Beth and Margaret with that one one evening when we were being poetic out in a field, after a school picnic, I think it was. Lapis lazuli wasn't popular, though. Beth came up with "Persian blue" a little later on, and we were impressed with "Persian blue." It was our very favourite colour for the longest time, and I really did feel quite outdone by Beth after that, until I found out that she'd gotten pencil crayons sent to her by her aunt in Toronto, and there was a colour in the pack called "Persian blue," and that's where she got it from. I don't try to give that look of the sky at dusk a name any more. It's the natural colour of the world, the original colour of the universe. I don't call anything "Persian blue" any more.

The owl reminds me of the first time I heard the fox bark late at night when I was sleeping on the porch on a hot night. It was one of the first nights I dared to sleep on the porch, away from my little room upstairs. I hadn't fallen asleep yet. Mosquitoes were getting through the screen somewhere, and I guess I was a bit afraid of — of a face appearing suddenly, I suppose. And then I heard that fox bark, a kit, probably, way out on the field of newly sprouted grain. It sounded unearthly. I'd never heard anything like it before. And I stepped quickly into the kitchen....

...and that's when I saw...Father sleeping with his hand on your shoulder....

I got used to the fox. Whenever I heard one barking in the night, I pictured him sitting on Father's stone and calling out to someone....

"I didn't know how I could possibly make it all the way back...."

I made it all the way back....

"Two people inside me were pulling at each other — leave, stay. I heard stories at the time about a girl — a girl I knew, who had a baby when I did, when I had you — who met a trucker at the bar in town one night, and the next morning packed a suitcase and took off with him in a Mac eighteen-wheeler, leaving husband and baby behind. And for some reason, I wanted to have the guts to do that. I wanted guts. I'd lost them all when I settled down here, settling, farming, having a baby, throwing fried potatoes and sausage skins to pigs, while your father went out every day and came back full of joy, even with those stones all over his land. You probably haven't ever thought of him as a joyful man.

"I couldn't explain that pulling inside me. But the evening that we walked together, I saw your father standing on the rock, in the field, turning around and around, looking over his crops like a man looking at the world from a mountain-top. And I don't think he even saw us, you and me standing there.

"All at once I felt about the settling dust of the evening the way I did about that big warm dust cloud that earlier afternoon in April—something was gone all wrong. And when you and I walked back to the house, I didn't hold your hand, even though you tripped on the green plants in the field. And you didn't cry when you fell, and you didn't ask for my hand."

But you've often held me and taught me things. I've sometimes learned important things from you in roundabout ways. I remember the day some girls from ninth grade came around selling jars of spices for a school project, and they were made up with orange lipstick and green eye-shadow and cakey, pastey mascara around their cold eyes. They were shy, I suppose, and they covered up with giggles and awkward gestures. I was younger than they were, but I suspect you saw a flush of envy on my face as they stood on the porch talking about their project. You turned to me, and a look crossed your eyes that was as unfamiliar to me as I suppose mine was to you.

And then you opened the jars one by one, and smelled the spices, and you talked on and on about how fresh and natural they smelled, and how well nature had provided the earth with beauty and perfumes. I thought it was odd — and they laughed at you.

And that evening when I came out of the bath, I stood before the mirror, and you came up behind me without saying a word, and took my wet hair in your hands and pulled it back from my face, and just held it like that. You didn't say anything — you just made me look at my own face, plain and naked.

When I started high school, I found out that the girls selling the spices were the ones who ran after boys. Some of these girls were smart in class, too, and even the teachers flirted with them. But when they put on their lipstick during breaks, and when they put on the eye-shadow that was supposed to make their eyes look soft and blue and innocent, they were putting on lies. I felt the coldness of those girls when they made tight circles to shut the rest of us out, and when they laughed at sad, shy boys who wore the wrong clothes.

"The next afternoon, Dad took you to town with him. I walked with you to the pick-up and stood by that old maple, the only tree left in the yard now, and waved good-bye to you as you drove off. You didn't see me waving.

"I went to the house and looked through all the photo albums, and I especially looked at the faces of my mother and grandmother, and then at the faces of their husbands, my father and grandfather. I looked for secret hardness in the women's eyes and joy in the men's. But those grey pictures didn't give anything away. I couldn't recognize any of their expressions. They all looked so grim. And in the end, when I'd finished, they were all just strangers, those cramped-in people with dry-creek eyes. To this day, I can't recall any of them ever having said anything real to me or to each other.

"Then I walked to the same place as we'd walked the evening before. I suppose the owl may have been there, sleeping somewheres in those willows, but I let him be, and just wandered around, beside the creek-bank, through the dry creek, scuffing up dust with my shoes. I came up along Kruegers' poplars. They were little trees then. There was a lot of silt drifted up against the row of poplars which I hadn't noticed the night before. As I walked there, I saw all kinds of marks in the soft dirt, mouse-tracks, bird-feet, insect-skitters.

"I saw something else. I stopped walking, and stared and stared, for quite a while, I think. You see, there were handprints in the soil-drifts, two hands, two little chubby hands, clear as could be, right in front of me, at my feet. I knelt down. I wanted to touch them, but didn't dare make even the slightest dent in them with my fingertip. And then I thought it was raining, because a drop fell and blackened a bit of dirt, and I was so glad that it was going to rain. But I remember worrying that the handprints would dissolve if it rained.

"Then I realized that I was crying. It wasn't raining at all, and didn't for a long time.

"I came back to this house with a joy of my own that day, that you'll never see in a family album, either. I didn't go back to look at the handprints again, because I was afraid that maybe the winds had carried them away. Maybe they wouldn't be there."

There are so many alone things here, aren't there? Ones of things? It would seem lonely to people like the girls who paint their mouths, girls in closed circles in school hallways; it would seem lonely to them not to have someone near by all the time who masked her eyes exactly the same way.

"Your father will be at the stone now, standing on it, probably, while he leans on the wooden stake and hammers it into the ground."

But all those solitary things stand beside one another, somehow, and keep a kind of company where there is no imitating one another's masks, where the colour of the summer sky before dark doesn't need a name. I understand why Father no longer keeps pigs on the farm — they don't belong in the oneness of life here. . . .

"I don't know why I told you this today — maybe to tell you why I didn't hold your hand that time, or so you won't wonder so much what's behind my face in all those old pictures. I wish you wouldn't go so soon. Just listen to that old fan!

"He'll be back soon from the field. He'll whistle when he comes down the driveway. I do believe this is more your father's world than it is mine or yours."

Go with him to the rock. Play "Blueberry Hill" with him.

"Have you ever heard the fox bark late at night?"

"Yes."

The No Place Bar and Grill

Kingdom, North Dakota huddled under the endless sky of flat northern farmland, its buildings herded together by relentless open spaces and grey whips of road. From the air, it did not seem so forlorn — other settlements were visible just at the place where the earth curved away. But the people of Kingdom usually forgot about the other places. Some wanted to forget, others simply could not remember.

Rita Leonard looked at the flat untilled field, still shiny in the low spots where the mud from early autumn rain had not quite dried. "Yes, that's perfect," she said. "He will sell, you say?"

"Yes, Rude's a pistol and a half, for such an old geezer. The idea of you building on his land fired him up, all right," said the real-estate man. "But what do you want to put it there for, right in the middle of no place?"

"I know lots of people who will drive miles and miles just to get to a no place like this," which wasn't quite true. Rita Leonard did not know very many people, and no one at all in North Dakota. She and her husband had come to Kingdom from Oklahoma to take over a strawberry farm and build a bar on Rude Faulkner's potato field.

The real-estate man turned a half-circle on the road. "Funny. The youngsters in this town are just scratching to get out and move to Fargo, and you say there are those who are scratching to get in."

Rita looked past his face at the field and squinted into a weak sun. "Nice thing about visiting no place is that you don't have to stay there."

"You say your husband's a pilot?"

"Crop-duster. Retired. He says there's too many things in the air these days." Truman Leonard felt his heart giving out and he dreamed about strawberries. But more than that, as he nosed up over power lines and poplar bluffs or surprised naked and terrified young men strapped into their ultralights, he felt like a tired commuter in rush-hour traffic. He was usually thinking about Artie, his son, who refused to lift off the ground by any mechanical means and had disappointed his father every minute of their lives together. Artie wanted to dance, to be a dancer. But where in Oklahoma could a thin boy with legs like snakes and hands like water lilies find a place to dance, except along river bottoms and on grass-covered knolls? After a day of draping lethal white shrouds on green carpets, Truman would soar out of the sunset over calm evening mists to see his son dressed in chiffon and satin, leaping about on the runway like a crazy person. Fabric floated like aphids' wings, and Truman wanted to pull the throttle that released the poison and exterminate the exotic insect. Last spring Artie had run away to New York to dance, and Rita and Truman had come nine hundred miles up through the corn country and the Badlands and sugar beet country to Kingdom, North Dakota to no place.

"Your husband's back in Oklahoma, you say?"

"Yes. He went to tie up our affairs there and bring his plane back. He decided to keep the plane a while, should be flying in tomorrow. Think we can get the foundation done before winter?"

"If it dries up real good."

And so the No Place Bar and Grill rose up from the potato field, interrupted by a five-month winter that oppressed Rita and Truman with its deadness and cold. Truman clung to his strawberry visions, Rita ordered the equipment for the bar and arranged for money.

In spring, among the rafters and beams of the wooden frame, the workers spoke of the Ezekialites, who had an enclave on the opposite side of town. The Ezekialites had lived in Kingdom for fifteen years, though they made no friends in town and sent only the adolescents to take care of business.

"Don't know how those Zekes are gonna take to a bar in their town," said a man with a hammer to Rita one morning. "They came here to Kingdom to escape from evil."

"Kingdom isn't their town," said Rita. "I hardly ever even see any of them. What do they believe in, anyway?"

"Weird things."

"Like what?"

"You'll see."

By May, the newest thing in town was the No Place Bar and Grill, and the oldest thing was the boarded-up grain elevator with chinks in the wood where knot-holes had disintegrated in the sun and wind and snow.

And Truman raked the straw off his fields and saw for the first time the plants that had slept there all winter and would soon rise from their bed and blink white-flower eyes at the brightening sky.

The Dance

The first day the bar was open, a young girl wearing a coarsely woven dress and cheap rubber thongs drove up to the off-sale window in an army jeep and bought eight bottles of rum. She didn't talk to Rita except to give her order, then paid and drove away. "That was a Zeke!" said Rude Faulkner. "What in hell are they going to do with that rum?" Every week, the girl returned to buy eight bottles of rum, one for each household in the Ezekialite colony.

The No Place Bar and Grill had no grill. Crop-dusting savings had not stretched that far. Rita's plans for Saturday-night bar-becues were put on hold for a year. But there was a platform in one corner for a band to play on, and beside it a smooth wooden floor for dancing. Rita and Rude Faulkner waltzed together to try out the space and the polished surface, though no music played. The jukebox had not yet arrived. "In one week, the musicians will be here," Rita announced to the opening-day patrons, most of whom were men. "Bring your sweethearts and come and dance." She drew posters and sent Rude's son, Abe, to the far-flung towns of the region to tack them up in stores and post offices.

The weather was Oklahoma hot, now that the soil had warmed up and the morning clouds floated away for the day. Truman irrigated the strawberry plants each night from a series of ponds dug by the previous owner, and he spent each day on the fields with a cluster of bare-legged children pulling thistles and nettles and dandelions from the rows of strawberries. Early every morning Truman flew over the Dakotan flatness to look at Kingdom from the air and at other towns, and sometimes at the Red River twisting along the Minnesota border. Sometimes he thought about Artie, but not very often. The sky was not so cluttered here, and he was free to soar well above tall structures and lines of trees and ultralights, instead of dodging obstacles fringing farmers' fields. Now he could fly as high as he could go. He rarely went to the No Place Bar.

The day the musicians were to come, Rita counted again the chairs and the bar stools and the tables, knowing how many there were as well as she knew the lines on her face, and fretted and paced on the dance floor about there not being enough room for patrons who would want to sit after long, warm dancing. She cursed the billiard table Rude had encouraged her to buy, for though it attracted the afternoon boys, it became a useless monstrosity on a busy night. She cursed Truman a little, too, because leaving Oklahoma behind was supposed to have instilled interdependence between them, survival and renewal. In Oklahoma, Truman had been sullen and unspeaking, even after Artie had left. In Kingdom, he was still unspeaking and uninvolved in Rita's new life, yet he was more serene, and when his airplane passed over No Place her heart still flew up to him fully, though she cursed him when he was on the ground.

Rita heard gunshots outside the bar. She hurried to a window and parted the slatted blinds, expecting to see blackbirds falling, or a black crow in tatters, like charred paper-ash. There was an army jeep on the road just down from No Place, towards the town. Two figures with rifles were picking up a corpse from the shoulder of the road. A small limp body swung from one man's hand as they walked through the heat waves rising from the roadbed.

"Zekes killing abominations," whispered Rude in Rita's ear, as though the men outside would hear. Rude always went into the bar through the rear service entrance because he fancied himself its owner, having raised potatoes on the ground underneath it year after year.

"They're hunting gophers," said Rita. "Lots of people around here hunt gophers."

"It's religious, for them. They hate all creeping things smaller than a dog. They gather up all their spiders and toads and mice and everything and burn 'em in their church. That's what they're going to do with that gopher."

"How do you know?"

"Everybody knows."

"There's probably a bounty on them."

"There is, there is! But the Ezekialites never collect it!"

"Maybe they eat them," said Rita, who did not like the mystery on the other side of Kingdom.

"And you know what? When they first came here, they bought an old lumber store to be their church. The name of the store was the Gopher Lumber Company. Went bankrupt. When the Zekes moved in, folks in Kingdom started calling it the Church of the Gopher Lumber. They built their colony around it."

The jeep floated away over the heat waves and eventually turned off onto a side road that led to the colony.

When the band came, Rita treated them like royalty, with broad gestures of her hand, nervous giggles, blushing, and offers of free beer. The band was mostly fiddlers, and Bob, the head fiddler, was a welder in Olympus, North Dakota, about twenty miles from

Kingdom. Seeing that the barmaid Rita had hired was just a homely Kingdom girl, he flirted with Rita's blushes and giggles, since there was little to tell bars apart except the women who worked in them. While his wife, the singer, fiddled with the microphone, Bob fiddled with Rita, telling her she had nice ears. She laughed, and he told her she had nice teeth. "Bob, we got a loose connection here," blared the microphone. Fiddler Bob winked at Rita and gave her a smile that had a toothpick in the corner of it, and sauntered back to the platform.

As the sun turned redder and redder in the suspended dust of Dakota air, more and more faces began to appear at the glass door of the No Place Bar and Grill. At first the faces were men's faces, field-tanned, unshaved, sometimes coated with dust. But when the fiddlers started to play, women's faces began to accompany the men's, women's faces brown and lined like their husbands'. They were shy at first, both men and women, and stood awkwardly at the door until hailed by cronies, or until they spotted an empty table. Abe Faulkner and Vivien, the girl Rita had hired to help out on busy nights, carried trays above the patrons' heads while Rita manned the taps behind the bar, taps that gushed bubbling, coloured liquids with a sound Rita could hear even above the drumbeats and the skirl of the fiddlers.

"Nobody's dancing," Rude muttered in Rita's ear as he helped himself to a pickled egg from the big jar beside the cash register.

"One beer will do it for most of them."

"That's Welder Bob from Olympus. Myrna could've done better. He knocks her around." The fiddlers played a waltz. "Let's dance, Reet. It would be fitting," said Rude, and he grabbed her hand and pulled her away from the taps. She pushed her hair up and away from her forehead as they zig-zagged towards the dance floor. They waltzed, Rude holding Rita tighter than he had in their tuneless rehearsals. His thin, elderly chest and thighs pressed against her. He moved his hand up and down her spine, caressing the plumpness of her back, his other hand, however, cupping her palm ever so lightly and courteously.

When they returned to the bar, Truman was sitting on a stool.

He looked like the other farmers in the place. Vivien was serving him a whisky.

"Truman, dance with me," said Rita. She wouldn't make a ceremony of his unexpected visit. He raised his eyes to her, then lowered them to his glass and said nothing.

People were dancing now, the men in baggy work-clothes, a few wearing overalls, the solid, large-hipped women wearing clean dresses that sat snugly on their hips and buttocks and then fell straight to their knees. The hems moved provocatively around the knees with the swaying of the hips and buttocks. There was style in the dancing, practised moves and grace, even though the men kept their caps on and held the women too tight.

At last, Truman reached for Rita's arm across the bar and said through stiff lips, "The berries got a fungus. A fungus. I didn't watch close enough." He took two greenish strawberries from his shirt pocket and laid them like dead kittens in front of Rita. "They weren't even ripe yet."

As he spoke, Rita saw behind him yet another face at the door, this one not like the others, this one pale and smooth as a vampire's, with large eyes and a sad mouth, and black hair sculpted carefully into a lock that overhung one of the large eyes. The face lingered at the door. "Truman," said Rita, "did it get all the berries?"

"Most," he replied.

"You can save them with chemicals or something, can't you?"

"It's too late."

"Don't you dare give up, Truman," said Rita as he ground the strawberries to a pulp with the bottom of his glass.

When he looked up again, he saw his face in the mirrored wall behind the bar, and he saw the back of Rita's hair, and he saw the face of his son moving across the room towards them. How like his mother he was, pale and dark. She'd been a stunner at eighteen.

Arthur Leonard said nothing. Truman Leonard said nothing. Rita Leonard went to the boy and said, "You're back." Then, to Rude Faulkner, she said, "This is my son Artie." And to Vivien and Abe she said, "This is my son Artie." Everyone in No Place stared at him, not only because of his pale skin and black hair and eyes, but also because he was wearing a black wool cape, though it was a warm evening.

Finally, when she asked, "How did you get here?" he answered, "Inside a dog with wheels. There's going to be a terrible storm. We saw lightning in the sky in that direction, whatever that direction is in this god-forsaken place. This place is more god-forsaken than Oklahoma, Mother. Whatever possessed you to come here?"

Truman made a move as if to slap the boy, but instead took hold of the collar of his cape and said through a false smile and clenched teeth, "So good to see you again, Son." Then he walked away and left through the back entrance.

"I see you're having a dance," said Artie.

When the rain began, it was a drizzle for an hour or so, but around midnight it pounded the potato field with a roar that could be heard through the high, screened windows of the bar. The dancers worried that their half-tons would be mired in the parking lot, so they left in a hurry, though the fiddles continued to play, leaving only the drunks and Rude and Vivien and Abe and Rita and Artie.

Abe and Rude had covered the billiard table with a sheet of plywood in the afternoon so that patrons could sit on it and put their drinks behind them. Some of the younger guests had sat on it for a while, until they could steal abandoned chairs. Now Artie threw off his cape and approached the table with a kind of reverence. Most of the musicians had stopped playing, but Welder-Fiddler Bob continued to fiddle a polka-like tune, slowly, like a record at half-speed. Artie walked around the plywood-covered pool table, all around it, and ran his slender hand along the rough edge of the wood. He leaped onto the table, landing in a crouching position, his snake-like legs folded beneath him. Then he straightened up. His white sleeveless T-shirt had *New York* written across the front and came down only past his rib cage so that his lean stomach showed. His pants were thin, close-fitting and black, tight at the waist and ankles. On his feet were black, hard-soled shoes.

Artie began to dance to the eerie half-speed polka, dancing not only with his feet, but with his whole body and his hands. Sometimes his moves mimicked the moves of the farmers he'd watched before the drizzle had turned to torrent. The tempo of the music gradually, almost imperceptibly, quickened. Faster and faster, until the plywood rumbled under Artie's feet like the thunder that was all around them now. The drunks woke to gaze at the apparition, the incarnated thunder writhing above the pool table. The dancing quickened the music, and the music quickened the dance.

The Fire

"Did you call him here?"

"No, I did not. I did not know where he was."

Rita and Truman lived in a house trailer under a cluster of cottonwoods at the edge of the potato field. They'd spent a cold winter there, and now they roasted inside the trailer like two chickens in an oven. It was Sunday morning. Artie was asleep on the roof, which was in shadow until noon. He'd stripped himself naked at dawn, wrapped himself in a sheet, and climbed to the top of the trailer, finding a dry place among the pools of rain on the uneven roof. Truman had taken a mickey of whisky with him when he left the bar and had drunk it through part of the night.

"Why'd he come back?"

"Things didn't happen fast enough in New York. He had no money. He doesn't know how to work. He didn't tell me everything, but he probably couldn't stick with a job. And you don't become a dancer overnight, even in New York."

"I'm gonna take a buzz around."

"Truman, you're still half drunk. You can't fly today."

But Truman pulled on his boots and left. The potato field hissed as the morning sun burnt off the rain, and a mist rose between the trailer and the No Place Bar and Grill. Artie sat up and watched his father make his way along a grassy verge to the road where his truck was parked.

A warm wind came up and Artie saw the plane coming before he heard it, a flash of white low in the sky. The wind blew its sound away until it was nearer and higher. Artie stood up, his sheet rippling, and the plane, now loud, soared over the cottonwoods towards the Red River. The wind carried the sound back to him for a long time.

"Is there a place to swim?" Artie asked his mother.

"There's a creek, but it belongs to the Ezekialites. You'll have to ask at the store in town."

"What's an Ezekialite?"

"It's hard to find out for sure what they are. Everybody makes up what they want them to be. But I wouldn't try to swim in their creek, if I were you." Then Rita laughed. "There's probably not a drop of water in it any more."

"How can North Dakota be so hot, Mother?"

"Truman's ponds still have water. You could swim there."

"Among strawberries."

On Monday morning, the girl in the jeep came to buy rum. "She's beautiful," said Artie after his mother had served her in their mute ritual.

"She's an Ezekialite. She doesn't talk."

"I want to find out her name."

Artie began spending the mornings in Kingdom, at the places where Ezekialites might go. He would walk to town, striding like a young Ichabod Crane along the shoulder of the road, often lost in dust from passing traffic. In town, he loitered in Gorman's Groceteria, in Kingdom Drugs and Gifts, in Nordak Hardware, at the Tastee Freez window, and he roamed around the few short streets. Little boys threw sticks at him.

Rita laid off Abe Faulkner and got Artie to help her in the afternoons, but he wasn't good at it. So often he was lost in his thoughts and preoccupied with his body. Rita kept him on, and prodded him with short, low-toned instructions. Vivien helped Rita evenings. The clientele were mostly complacent regulars, still mostly men, who got used to Artie's leaps from flamboyance to sullenness and back. Truman came in more often, and drank more. On the nights when they had dances, both Vivien and Artie served customers, but Truman still refused to dance with Rita. After midnight, Artie danced on the billiard table, alone. The strawberries softened underneath the warm, wet fungus spreading from plant to plant.

"Thing about the Zekes," said Rude Faulkner to Rita one afternoon, "is that they keep all those cows partly because they cook and heat with dung. Collect it and dry it somehow. Keeps 'em busy. But they don't sell the meat or the milk to anyone in town that I know of. Some say they burn cattle for sacrifices. I don't believe that, though. You'd smell it."

"Doesn't anyone know any truths about these people?" Rita asked.

"They don't live truth-like. Book of Ezekial's all full of dreams and visions and symbolic acts. There's no pattern for day-to-day life there. Seems to me your son'd make a good Zeke."

On a humid night towards the end of June, while the patrons of the No Place Bar and Grill slouched over their tables of beer and drawled about how the weather was good for the crops and about fishing trips to Canada and about tornadoes in Texas, the pleasant smell of smouldering wood wafted through fan-churned air. There was a juke-box now, and it was playing *Seven Spanish Angels*. Vivien was playing rummy in between looking after customers. In the store-room at the back, Rita sorted cartons of liquor. At first, the smell seemed so much a part of the night air that no one paid attention to it. Then, at the same moment, Rita came out of the store-room and Truman came bursting through the front door. "What's that smell?" said Rita to the air. "The roof's on fire!" said Truman to the bar.

"Who puts out fires in Kingdom?" Rita asked Rude Faulkner as she picked up the telephone.

"Olympus. Just tell the operator. But I'd start wetting down the roof if I were you."

Some of the patrons got up from the tables and ambled out to the mercury-lit yard to see the smoke twisting out of the eaves, but most stayed in the bar with their tall glasses. The fire did not seem to be spreading very fast, though smoke was now evident inside the bar. At the table, the men made bets as to how long it would take for the Olympus fire department to get to Kingdom.

"Wait a minute," said Rita, beginning to panic. "There's no water anywhere nearby to put out a fire, except the little that's in our well!"

"They bring a big tank, maybe two. You better hope to hell it's not gonna be a big fire," said Rude. "Must be electrical." The men who'd gone out to look came in for refills and went back out to listen for sirens and watch for winking red lights. Someone had put a ladder to the roof and was sloshing trashbags filled with water over the part near the smoke. The bags were brigaded by Rita and Vivien and Rude. Truman had disappeared.

The firemen were there in half an hour, with hatchets. First they examined the roof. Then they went inside and examined the ceiling. "You're lucky the wood's new and it's been so humid," they told Rita. The bar patrons drank their beer and told fire stories.

Artie came running through the front door, breathless. "I know her name!" he said to Rita, who was looking at the ceiling with the firemen. "She told me her name. She is beautiful, Mother. Her name is Buzi. She told me her name." He paced alongside the bar, combing his hair back from his sweating forehead, destroying the sculpture of the forelock. But Rita's mind was on the wires smouldering in her roof. She barely noticed him.

The firemen from Olympus stayed a long time afterward to make sure the fire did not revive. They drank free pop and complained about how hot it was inside their uniforms.

The Fourth of July

"Back in Oklahoma, we had big wheatfields," said Truman Leonard to the group of Ezekialite children who picked the untainted berries in the least affected patch. "Wheatfields bigger than all of North Dakota. They were bright yellow, and when you flew over one of those fields, it was like flying over a gold satin sea, and if you dipped your wings, you could make that wheat roll like a regular ocean." The children didn't look at Truman or answer him, but they couldn't block out his words. "And then the custom combiners would come and mow it all down in straight cuts and truck it all off. There're grain elevators in Oklahoma just like the one in Kingdom, except not old or boarded up, and sometimes there's piles of grain lying all around the elevator like piles of yellow pearls. I wished to have me a wheatfield, but I wished more for ripe, red strawberries. When I met my wife, she had strawberry juice all around her mouth.

"My boy has never flown over one of those wheatfields. He's never flown with me at all. I bet you'd like to fly in the plane, wouldn't you? The Red River here is just like the Canadian River in Oklahoma, just snaking along like that. Wouldn't you like to fly in my plane? I'll take you for a ride." The children had strawberry juice around their mouths. They all wore the same coarse tunics and had yellow hair. They put berries into home-made baskets.

"In Oklahoma, everybody started to fly. Pretty soon you couldn't go nowhere without running into kites and hang-gliders and power lines and oil derricks, and planes, planes, planes. C'mon, I'll take you for a ride." Truman reached for one of the children and they all ran away.

"This cloth is too rough for your pretty skin. Aren't you allowed to wear smooth satin, Buzi, and let your hair grow long and put glass slippers on your feet?" The grain dust in the old elevator had long settled, and though the air smelled dark and sweet, it was clean, and swam with town smells coming through chinks and knotholes. Artie's hands fluttered along Buzi's neck and arms while rats stirred beneath the old wooden floor.

"Let me tell you the story of Cinderella. I'll tell you fairy tales and you can tell me the parables of Ezekial. Every time I see you, I'll tell you a fairy tale and you tell me a Bible dream.

"Once upon a time, there was a prince who loved to dance, and he searched his whole life for a princess wearing glass slippers.

Take off your rubber thongs, Buzi. Here. And he sent his magician, Horton, to search for the dancing princess with glass shoes. Horton searched all of the world for such a creature, and finally came to North Dakota on an airplane made of silver and gold with jewelled wings and mirrored windows and he found a dirty, black-haired girl dancing with a broom in a potato bin, and all the potatoes watched her with their white beady eyes. Her name was Cinderella and Horton fell in love with her. He didn't like North Dakota, but was mad for the skyscraper palace of his dear Prince. Since he was mad for Cinderella as well, he knew that the only way he could be near her would be to deliver her to his master, the Prince, as the princess with glass slippers.

"They flew home and when they got there he made her a royal coach out of a potato and spun her a dress out of strawberry leaves." Artie caressed Buzi's feet. Each time a rat whimpered or clawed wood, she started and caught her breath, and Artie shushed her and smoothed her hair. "Of course the Prince was mad for her, too. Horton allowed him to have Cinderella to dance with every evening, but Horton told Cinderella that her dress would turn to nettles and her shoes to rubber if she didn't come back to him every night at midnight. This wasn't true, but it didn't have to be. Cinderella came to him faithfully at midnight every night, and Horton loved her. Don't be afraid, Buzi. Let me kiss you." The frightened girl scrambled to her feet and ran to the loose boards in the wall through which they'd climbed together earlier that morning. She was gone in an instant.

On the Fourth of July, Rita built a large pen beside the No Place Bar and Grill with a few rolls of snow-fencing, and called it a beer garden. She set up picnic tables and strung coloured lights from corner to corner on tall wooden poles. Rude Faulkner spent the day helping her build the garden while Artie worked inside. There were more customers than usual because of the holiday, and Artie was more bemused than usual in a loose red silk shirt he'd found at a second-hand shop in Olympus.

Vivien arrived late in the afternoon and the beer garden

officially opened for business. It was on the shady side of the bar and the air was drier than in June.

"Truman's been flying drunk," Rude told Rita as they installed a keg of draught in a corner of the beer garden. "Think he wants to kill himself?"

"He hasn't got any self-respect anymore. And he won't let me touch him. He watches his berries rot every day. He's sold some, but he just hasn't got any heart left, Rude. Think I should tell 'em to take his licence away?"

"He'd probably fly without it. That's the kind of slough he's in. You know, I've never seen him talk to the boy there."

"I guess I made him too much — my boy." Rita had never said those words out loud, not even to her neighbours in Oklahoma.

"Why, he's not like you at all," said Rude.

"No, he came out a butterfly. Sometimes I wonder if I breathed in too much of Truman's poison when I was carrying him. I was thirty years old. I wish he could be a dancer."

"Would you like to get rid of him?"

"I'd like him to be rid of us."

When Rita went to the store-room for plastic cups, she found Truman kissing Vivien among the fireworks Rude was going to set off after nightfall. The girl was not struggling. "Have your last hurrah, Truman," said Rita. "You're fifty and I'm forty-nine, and you wish you were flying through a clear sky with a clear mind and I wish you'd become tall again and ask me to dance. This may be the last hurrah for both of us."

Welder-Fiddler Bob was back with his band. He winked and drawled at Rita but she could no longer blush or laugh at his attentions. The patrons had to dance in the dirt.

Everyone moved out of the enclosure to the larger space behind the No Place Bar and Grill to watch the fireworks away from the lights. A quarter moon gleamed in the centre of the purple night sky, and it was towards that moon that Rude Faulkner, on his half-ton truck far out on the flat field, aimed his rockets. Artie lay on his back, and through the popping and crackling and snarling of Rude's light show, he spoke to Rita.

"They worship storms. Lightning bolts are swords of God, thrust from the sky to remind them that He is the Father. During thunderstorms they blow trumpets to answer, like angels. I would like to be there, listening to the trumpets and the thunder." The sky burst into red, white, and blue. "Have you seen their bracelets, Mother, their silver bracelets? When the girls are twelve years old, they each get a bracelet welded onto their right arm as a symbol of salvation from harlotry. They can't wear any other jewellery or make-up or satiny clothes, or be with men, or the bracelet is cut off and they are put out onto the road at night and not allowed back in ever again."

"Did the girl tell you these things, Artie?"

"Every year in summer they celebrate the Feast of Gog, and everyone dresses in linen and is handed a paper scroll by the priest, and they eat the paper, Mother, and wash it down with sheep's blood. And they eat the meat of young calves and lambs and goats — fatlings, she called them. There are other things they do on the Feast day, but she didn't want to tell me about them yet." Green and pink sparkled against the white moon.

"Anyone who disobeys is silenced with a cloth tied around his mouth and has his hands tied behind his back and must lie in a corner for three hundred and ninety minutes, and must then go to the temple to pray for forty minutes. They believe in omens. The priests and priestesses read sheep livers for prophecy."

"Rude said something about them killing small animals."

"Animals other than what they use for food and rituals are abominations because they can become idols and false gods. Animals must all die at the hands of men. It's a belief in domination, Mother. Their language is full of words like *harlotry* and *idolatry*." When Rita looked at her son, his face glowed with moonlight and as the fireworks exploded above, the colours shone in his eyes and in the fair skin of his cheekbones. He was radiant.

"They believe in fire and brimstone. How afraid they might be of the Fourth of July!" He laughed. "Ezekial had dreams, Mother, visions. He had a connection with God, so that all his dreams were important and had meaning." Many of Artie's words were lost

among the explosions below the moon, but these were the words
he said:

"Ezekial had a dream about a valley full of bones, dry, dead
bones. He lands in this valley as if he'd flown there like an angel.
God tells him to prophesy that the bones will rise and grow flesh
and hair and sinew, and he does it, and up they come out of the dust,
thousands of bones, rattling and popping like firecrackers, I would
think. But they're still corpses, with dry white skin and blind eyes.
And then God tells Ezekial to prophesy life into them, and he does,
and blood and life rush into the dead bodies and they all begin to cry
out and there's a tremendous wailing and noise in the valley,
echoing from mountain to mountain." Artie laughed into the red
tendrils of fire falling down from the sky. "I wish I could have been
there. I wish I could have seen it and I wish my dreams were as
beautiful as that."

The Fight

When Rita told Rude what her son had told her, he said, "I
don't know. He could have gotten all that just from reading the
Bible. I don't know. What do you think? Did he make it up?"

"I don't know."

"One thing: if that Zeke is really talking to him about this stuff,
she's in for it. They'll strip her naked and chuck her out of one of
their jeeps some cold night in winter. Happened once before."

"Will they go after Artie?"

"Naw. But he'll feel like he killed her."

There weren't always voices in the abandoned grain elevator.
Sometimes when the little boys with sticks listened at the gap in the
boards, the only sounds they heard were rats scratching in the walls
and sparrows twittering and occasionally the yelping of the wind in
the knotholes.

"Where does he go?" Truman asked Rita one morning as he
watched the tall boy making smooth strides along the road. Artie's
red shirt was tied by the sleeves around his neck so that it hung
on his shoulders like a cape, and his white face was shielded by a

black-brimmed hat.

"To town."

"What for?"

"He has friends there."

"Friends? In Kingdom?" Truman sat down on the step of the house trailer with an empty whisky bottle dangling from his thumb.

Rita stood behind him in the doorway and stared at the No Place Bar and Grill. She'd fired Vivien the day after the Fourth of July, but she still had Truman. Looking from the Bar and Grill to the listless swinging of the bottle, she said, "We've got to resurrect this family somehow, Truman. Do you think we should go back to Oklahoma?"

"I don't know," he answered.

"Why did we come here? You wanted to come here, to get away. What was it? Do you really know?"

Truman didn't answer until Artie was out of sight. Then he said, "I wanted to freeze the poison out of my veins. I wanted to see snow falling instead of pesticide. And I really wanted Artie to come back to us, here. But I wanted him to come back different." A dragonfly with wings clicking landed on Truman's knee. Its blood-coloured body was long and slender and virile. Straight wings intersected the body near the head. "I wanted to teach him how to fly. Why does he have such a hatred for my airplane?"

"He flies very well without you," said Rita. "You have hatred of your own."

It was August. The land was cooling off. Kingdom was surrounded by thick dark fields of sugar beets and potatoes, and taller fields of sunflowers and corn. In the town, someone threw broken glass into the wading pool in the park that was the pride and joy of the town council, and children cut their feet because the clear splinters of broken Coke bottles looked like shimmers of water. And on the Ezckialite colony, it was rumoured, a truck drove over a baby who had crawled under its wheel when no one was looking.

Everyone talked about those things in the bar. The eruption of injury, death in the small community brought a day or two of fear to Rita's patrons, a day or two of philosophizing and subdued voices.

On Rita's forty-ninth birthday, a thunderstorm moved in from Montana around nine o'clock in the evening. Truman had come into the bar drunk just before the storm struck. Rita was drinking more than usual. The few men in the bar toasted Rita over and over, and the beer was free in honour of the occasion. Welder-Fiddler Bob was there alone. He kept a beery hand on Rita's hip throughout the storm, as though the thunder had granted him special privilege.

Only Artie remained unaffected by liquor. He had given his mother a gold charm bracelet with a gold ballet slipper charm, and when he wasn't preparing and serving drinks, he fondled the bracelet on her arm, and grinned at the clink of the slipper on the wooden surface of the bar as she raised and lowered her sloe gin fizz.

"Where's that girl?" asked Welder-Fiddler Bob. "That used to work here."

"Vivien," said Rita. "I had to get rid of her."

"She went to Olympus," said Artie. "She is a harlot there, for twenty dollars."

Welder-Fiddler Bob laughed. "She's hooking in Olympus? For twenty bucks?" He laughed long and hard. "How come I don't know about it?"

Someone was asking Truman about his strawberries, though the season was over. "Rotten, rotten, and full of ants and crickets and aphids," he growled.

"It was just a simple rot. He could have gotten rid of it with fungicide," said Rita.

"Buzi said the strawberries tasted like rain and honey." Artie had come from behind the bar and stood beside Rita with his elbow on her shoulder.

"Buzi who?" slurred Truman.

"She's an Ezekialite," said Rita.

"You're messing with one of them Zekes?" exclaimed Welder-

Fiddler Bob.

Truman was on his feet.

"Messing?" The rain and honey had turned to acid in Artie's mouth.

"She talks to you?" said Truman in a clear, sober voice.

At first, it seemed as though a bolt of lightning had sliced through the roof of the No Place Bar and Grill and struck Artie's head. He fell back among chair legs on the carpeted floor. His father's face, dark red, slack-lipped, with hatred in his drunken eyes, glowered over him. It was an ugly face. "Mother — Mother —" Artie gasped.

But Rita did not go to her son. From her position on the bar stool, she kicked out with her high-heeled birthday shoe and caught Truman in the stomach. His body twisted away with the pain, and Rita, taking him off-balance, wrestled him to the ground, face down, where she smashed her fist against the back of his head several times. Artie remained on the floor, his long legs and arms bent like aphids' legs.

Welder-Fiddler Bob put his arm around Rita's waist and pulled her away. As soon as Rita's weight was off him, Truman slithered away and rocked to his feet and headed for the door without showing his face to the others again.

And then, Artie was up off the floor and running through the tables towards the retreating Truman. He leaped onto his father's back. "Aaaaagh!" he screamed into his father's ear, because he had no words for dealing with cataclysm. "Aaaaagh!"

Truman steadied himself by putting his hands on the back of a chair, but when Rita threw herself on the bodies of her husband and son, Truman fell at last to the floor, face down again, and Artie's screams rose to a high-pitched wail that replied to the swords of God thrust from heaven.

The Captives

When Rude Faulkner returned from a funeral in Olympus at 10:30 that evening, he found the back door of No Place locked. As

he came around the front of the building, he saw through a window
Artie's head bobbing above the pool table inside. The *Closed* sign
was up on the front door and it, too, was locked. Rude went back to
the window and watched the top half of Artie Truman. No music
played, but Rude could hear a faint rumbling somewhere, which
could have been the retreating storm, or Artie's feet on plywood.
He could see no one else in the bar.

Rude Faulkner had grown up in Centreville, South Dakota,
where there was a small hotel on Main Street run by a husband and
wife and son. The hotel rooms were seldom used, but the bar was
popular. The husband and wife and son were alcoholics, and the
only time the bar ever closed early was when the three of them got
into a family brawl, which happened regularly. Standing outside
No Place now, Rude stroked his bristly jaw and wondered if — no,
felt sure that something like that had happened now. He
considered walking across the field to the Leonards' trailer to find
out, but the house trailer was dark. Rude was tired from the day
spent in mourning, like so many other death days, coming more
frequently in his old age. He went home and slept.

At 7:30 A.M., Rita Leonard freed herself from the flaccid,
twisted sheets of their bed and threw open the door of the trailer to
look for air. She felt as twisted inside as the bedsheets. Truman had
woken at dawn with an intense passion to which they'd both
succumbed equally and fully, though they'd not begun the night
together. It had taken great physical strength to get Truman to the
house trailer last night. He'd wanted to go to his plane, to fly, but
Rita had struggled with all her might to keep him back. Finally,
Welder-Fiddler Bob had helped her drag him to the trailer, where
they'd thrown him onto the sofa and drenched him with a pitcher
of lemonade from the refrigerator. Rita had stayed with him and
held him down until he fell asleep.

As she stood there, looking out the door and letting the morning coolness cleanse her lemony, sticky skin, Rita felt afraid. Could
it have been the violence that had driven Truman at dawn — her
shoes in the pit of his stomach? Or the release of long-harboured

doubts and worry and pain and jealousy, all behind that single blow to Artie's face? Or was it that having drifted away from their love during the past year, he'd suddenly found himself still tethered to it and had snapped back with relieved joy? The first idea made her feel ashamed, the second nervous and fearful, the last profoundly sad and full of love at the same time.

Artie had slept in the bar. She watched him emerge from No Place and begin his walk to Kingdom.

Later in the morning, Artie came back from Kingdom, only this time he was running as he had the day he'd discovered Buzi's name. He ran half-crying and pounding the air with clenched fists. But before he reached No Place he heard his father's plane and saw it flying low dead ahead. The wheels of Truman's white airplane touched the dirt road. The plane roared along the road. Artie sobbed once and cut through the ditch as his father came to a standstill outside the bar.

"Mother — Mother — it's Buzi — they — all of them — she —"

"They've thrown her out."

Truman was at the door. "Arthur. We are going to fly now. Once. Come to the plane."

"No! It was their Feast Day — she was all covered, Mother, draped with — something — and her hair —" The words tumbled out in a rapid monotone, like a chant.

"They all cut off all their hair, all of it. When I saw Buzi today, her head was cleanshaven. It was covered with a linen sheet, but I took it off and all that was left of her was her beautiful eyes. Every Feast Day they shave off all their hair, and for three months they drape their heads with white linen. I — I don't know why. I wanted to save her, Mother. She was afraid. I wanted to take her with me. But she wouldn't come. I tried to force her into the jeep so we could drive away from Kingdom, but I didn't know how to drive the jeep, and she cried and said she had to stay. It's me she is afraid of."

"Son, you are going to fly with me if I have to strap your dead body to the fuselage."

Artie bolted for the back door, but Truman grabbed his arms

from behind and pushed him in the direction of the plane. "No! Dad — I'm — I'm scared. Please don't make me. I'm afraid to. Mother?"

This time Rita did not rescue him.

"I've been afraid of you all my life," said Truman and shoved him towards the plane. "So you're afraid to fly. Well, I'm going to make you really scared, Son, for the first time in your life. If you don't get up there I'll kill you," he said. Then he let go of his son's arms.

Artie's whimpers died away. He stood on the ground for a moment with his head bowed, then climbed up to the wing.

"We'll find us a big wheatfield," gloated Truman as they taxied along the road. "We may have to fly to Montana to find one, but we'll find one, and I'll show you a gold satin sea that rolls like a regular ocean."

Artie sat behind his father in the tiny cockpit with his head pressed against the rigid window beside him. He quivered and took short breaths. His eyes were closed.

"You must stop seeing her, Artie," said Rita. "If they find out, they cut her out, even from her family. You can't answer all her needs."

"She was beautiful without her hair, Mother."

"Forget her."

"I almost froze to death in New York, Mother. Did I tell you that? I nearly froze with no place to sleep one night. I have been terrified. He said I hadn't been. But I have. I have."

"Did you go high enough to see the earth curving away?"

"Yes."

"Did you see it?"

"I told him I did. I had my eyes closed most of the time."

August is a time of sunsets. Just before harvest begins, the air is kept pure by the thick crops holding down the soil and the sun has begun to soften in colour. As it sets, the western sky is rainbowed in hues of farm-fresh jellies, strawberry, saskatoon, and muskmelon. Later in August, the threshing dust from Montana and Saskatchewan drifts high into the atmosphere and the sun sinking into it swells into a soft balloon the colour of sloe gin. Thunderstorms are over. The season of cool rain begins.

Truman Leonard flies alone through the sunsets. Rita tends the bar, her gold bracelet and gold ballet shoe jingles and clicks on the countertop. Artie has run off to be a dancer, in California this time, where he can sleep outside in winter, and every Monday morning the girl named Buzi picks up eight bottles of rum in an army jeep. On Saturday nights, Welder-Fiddler Bob plays his fiddle and flirts with the women while Truman and Rita waltz on the wooden dance floor of the No Place Bar and Grill.

Lady-O

London Bridge is falling down,
Falling down,
Falling down.
London Bridge is falling down,
My fair Lady-O!
Oh! Oh! Yeeeeah!

"Willie, clap! Willie! My song is over and you said you'd clap. Come on!" The red skipping rope snaked across the threadbare grey carpet. Its loose end bounced where the rough edges on the handle caught on the rug. The tousled blonde in the white batwing sunglasses held the other handle in her fat hand. "Mother, my song is over and Willie said she'd clap and she didn't."

"My name isn't Willie."

Maggie's hands were in peas. Without looking up, she tightened the rubber band that held her pony-tail. Her hands were wet. "Willa's reading. Leave her alone."

Willa was reading *Marjorie Morningstar* and wished she lived in New York in an apartment block called the El Dorado, instead of on a farm in boring old Alberta. She could see her mother in the kitchen, stuffing fistsful of fresh peas from the sink into plastic bags. Peas were flying. Last year, her mom had acted as though peas were jewels. She'd glowed all through garden season. Willa remembered watching her do magic tricks with vegetables the whole summer long. Now she was throwing peas around like she'd found hairs in the sink.

"She promised!"

"She clapped for you three times before, Bridgit, now let her read her book. You can pretend."

With her free hand, Bridgit kicked up the long blue slip and pulled at the straps to bring the lace cups up a little closer to her flat chest. "You always take her side." She slumped over to where Willa was lying on the studio couch. The heels of her mother's bridesmaid shoes tangled in the skipping rope. "Willie-Willa, put the Helen Reddy record on. I want to sing 'Brian's Song' now. And you clap this time, okay?"

"Bridgit!" It was the kitchen voice.

"Please?"

Willa rolled off the red velvet studio couch. She loved the studio couch, even though it was old and didn't fit with the rest of the furniture in the farmhouse. It would definitely suit the El Dorado. "All right, Sarah Bernhardt." She'd gotten the name from *Marjorie Morningstar.*

Bridgit pulled up the skirt of the slip and stepped onto the vinyl ottoman in the centre of the living room. She held the skipping rope handle to her mouth, parted her lips, and waited for the intro. "That's not 'Brian's Song.' Willie, change it!"

Willa had put on their grandmother's Louis Armstrong record and gone into the kitchen. "Mom, can I wear lipstick when we go to Uncle Billy's this afternoon?"

"Me too! Me too!" Bridgit shouted. She kicked the oversized shoes at the living room window and leaped off the ottoman. "And red nail polish, and can I wear my new dress?" She was at the kitchen sink, delving with quick fingers into the peas they'd picked and shelled together earlier that morning.

"You'll have to let me finish or we'll not be able to go at all."

But Willa knew they had to go. Her mother had some kind of

appointment in town, probably something to do with their dad going away. Willa also knew he hadn't gone only to visit his sick mother in Victoria. The day he'd left, she had seen him stack all his tools in the station wagon. Even though they lived on a farm, they weren't farmers. They lived beside the Vermillion River where her father built canoes, and Maggie worked part-time in a crafts shop in town. Dad wouldn't take his wood-working tools on a trip to see his sick mother. And he'd taken most of his clothes, too, including his T-shirt with the breasts painted on the front, which he loved but never wore. Why would he pack it for a trip to Victoria?

"Why don't you both go outside and play with Barbra Streisand?" said Maggie. "She's been lonely since we sold her puppies."

"Mom, you're so weird," said Willa. She zipped up the tops of the freezer bags. "Nobody calls her that. Sarah Bernhardt calls her Barbra and I call her Sandy 'cause Barbra's a dumb name for a bassett hound." She held up one of the plastic bags and pressed it to her eyes and looked at her mother's face. "Dad calls her Barbie."

"Well, you named her."

"I did not! Bridgit did."

"It stinks outside," said Bridgit. "Skrypetzes cleaned out their pig barn this morning. Sybil says it desecrates the silk."

"You don't even know what desecrates means, Miss Bernhardt."

"Don't call her Sybil," said Maggie. "She's your grandmother. It's disrespectful."

Bridgit's mouth was full of peas and when she talked green slime oozed over her bottom lip. "She said we were soul-mates and I should call her Sybil. And I asked Daddy and he said it was all right. Let's go look at the lipstick, Willie-Willa."

Willa hoped she would meet a handsome thin boy named Noel in junior-high. All the boys in grade school were named Jake or Nestor or Bobby. She liked Noel.

Maggie's brother, Billy, had been a diamond-driller up north for the last ten years. Willa hardly knew him. He didn't come to see them very often. But he'd finally quit diamond-drilling and bought a little house in town. Three weeks ago he'd brought Willa and Bridgit mukluks and announced that he'd be receiving callers as soon as he was moved in. He'd winked at the girls, meaning that they were supposed to be the callers.

The three passengers in the dusty pick-up truck popped up and down on the seat as the truck rattled over washboard roads. Maggie had brushed out her pony-tail. The wind from open windows blew her hair into a swirl around the top of her head. Willa had pink lipstick on her lips and *Marjorie Morningstar* on her lap, an old, black, hard-covered copy with part of the spine ripped away. Bridgit sat very still in the middle, not wanting to disturb many things: her hair, crafted by Maggie's hands into a tight bun on the top of her head; her white dress, gathered at the waist with a pink ribbon; her red nail polish, not quite dry; her pink plastic beads, a gift from Sybil last birthday. They had nine miles to drive and seven of them were in silence.

"When is Sybil coming?" Bridgit's high-pitched voice rose over the grinding of the engine. Willa wanted to cover her ears. She knew what her mother would say.

Maggie recited the answer. "Grandma will come when she's well again. When Daddy comes back from Victoria he'll tell us how she's feeling and when she'll be coming to visit you and Willa and Barbra Streisand and the goats. And maybe she'll read to you from your new poetry book."

Why doesn't she tell the truth? thought Willa. The real answer was that Sybil was dying of cancer and would never come to visit them again. And if they ever did see her again, she would be in a high white bed with dead roses beside it. Willa heard plenty when reading late at night.

"And will she bring her gold shawl with the scarlet fringes?" asked Bridgit.

"I'm sure she will."

"And her silver whisky flask? And will we have wine with dinner when she's here?"

"We will have wine. You will have ginger ale."

Willa couldn't stand it any more. "I'm having Miss Hildebrandt for a teacher next year. She said we're going to do origami in class." One more year till junior-high, one more year and she wouldn't have her sister haunting her.

"We're doing origami in grade three and we're making Japanese fans with glitter sprinkled on them in a design and we're going to see a play in the city. We're taking a bus, not just cars like you did last year, Willie."

"I had Mrs. Hart in grade three, too, and we never did origami, and she never took us to a play. And how do you know you'll make Japanese fans? You always make stuff up. And my name isn't Willie."

"You wet your pants in assembly one time, I know that."

Willa turned towards the door and opened her book. The words blurred. What was *Pygmalion?*

"Mother, don't drive with your eyes closed," said the blonde with the red fingernails.

Billy's house was snuggled up against the back of the new supermarket. The house was small, more like a cottage, but it had a diamond-shaped window high above the front door, a window Bridgit and Willa noticed right away. Whenever Willa thought about Uncle Billy these days, she was reminded of Billy in *Marjorie Morningstar.* Marjorie's parents didn't like him because he was fat and awkward. Uncle Billy was sort of fat, but everyone seemed to like him.

"Mom, what's a hippie?" asked Willa as they parked in front of the little house. "Some kids in school said their parents said we were hippies."

"Short for hippopotamus," said Bridgit.

"Don't worry, it's nothing bad," Maggie said.

"They said it like it was bad." Willa and Bridgit and Maggie walked across the lawn to the front door.

"Mother, the truck is on. You forgot to switch it off. Can I do it?"

Maggie put her hand on the back of Bridgit's head. "I can't stay.

You can spend some time with Uncle Billy while I do some errands."

Since when is getting a divorce an errand? thought Willa. And what's with this *errands*, anyway? Maggie never said *errands*. She always said she had to do *stuff*. *Errands* was a word the school principal would use. Willa felt the tears coming up again.

Maggie reached for the doorbell but another finger was already there.

"Do you think he'll let us play in the attic?" whispered Bridgit. "You said he has an attic."

Through the screen door they saw a shaggy beard and a bald head and a pair of wire-frame glasses floating towards them in a dark hallway. Billy opened the door and wordlessly ushered them in. His chef's apron wasn't very clean. He wasn't wearing a shirt, and below the hem of the apron his hairy legs were bare, too. Maggie walked around him, looking at his apron and the back of his denim cut-offs, and laughed. "Is this your customary baby-sitting uniform?" she asked. She wore a white suit. "What do you do with children, cook them in wine with mushrooms and a bay leaf?"

Willa stared at her mother. She hadn't kidded around for weeks, years it seemed. Bridgit flung her sweater onto the arm of a chair and peeked into other rooms in the house. Billy and Maggie walked out onto the front porch, leaving Willa standing in the hallway. They didn't want her to hear. She put her book on the chair beside the sweater and followed Bridgit.

A card table for a desk. Pink swans on the shower curtain. A shrivelled cactus that looked like a cucumber. A price tag hanging from a lamp shade. And then, "Do you think this leads to the attic?" Willa stood in front of a closed door and spoke directly to it.

Bridgit jostled Willa aside and yanked on the old-fashioned crystal doorknob. A staircase led down, a steep, narrow staircase with old wooden steps. At the bottom of the stairs light glimmered through a dirty little window. "It stinks," said Bridgit.

It desecrates the silk.

Only one other door. Willa opened it with a cautious turn of her hand. This stairway led up. Billy and Maggie were still talking on the porch. "It's dark up there," whispered Bridgit.

"Maybe there's a light switch at the top." Willa tiptoed up the first few steps. They groaned as if in pain.

" 'Bye, girls! I'm off!" Maggie called from the front hall. Bridgit ran to her mother.

The steps creaked less the higher Willa got, and the passage grew brighter. Her head came up above the floor level of the attic. The low-ceilinged space was lit by the diamond-shaped window at one end, grey with dust like the one in the basement. The air was hot and smelled papery. Boxes, lots of cardboard boxes, all closed, littered the attic floor.

Willa could hear Bridgit down below. "I love you, Mother, and don't stay away long." She pictured her sister wrapped around Maggie, red fingernails digging into the back of the white suit.

Going down, Willa met Bridgit at the door. "What's up there?"

"It's real dark. And there's no light switch."

"Well, girls, how about some pizza?" Billy rubbed his hands together. "I was just about to make a nice big juicy one in a round pan. We'll save some for Maggie." He led them to the kitchen. "Bridgit, how are you at patting out dough? Those hands look like they'd be able to smack it real good." He pulled tin cans and cellophane packages out of a paper bag. "Willa, you can slice the pepperoni. And please don't get your finger mixed in with it. I tasted one once in a stew. It was terrible!" They all made faces and laughed.

Bridgit said, "I can cut things. My mother lets me at home. Willie, give me the knife."

While Bridgit sawed the meat into various shapes, Willa and Billy explored the refrigerator. "This used to be pineapple chunks," he explained. "Now it's a laboratory experiment. I'm trying to find a vaccine to cure mai-tai hangovers." He opened the jar lid.

"Yuk," said Willa.

Billy put the jar back in the fridge. "I've got mushrooms and green peppers."

"Are those grapes a laboratory experiment?" asked Willa. "Let's put them on the pizza."

"Yuk," said Bridgit.

"How about on half the pizza?" Billy ran his fingers through the curly fringe of hair above his ear. "Better cut 'em in half so they don't explode in the oven."

The half-grapes looked like big black beetles. "Beetle pizza," said Willa.

While they chopped and sliced and sprinkled, they talked about Sybil's rings, and pierced ears, and Sybil's cigarette-making machine, and school, and their favourite foods, and Sybil's fox collar. "Do you know my grandmother?" Bridgit asked.

"I met her at your parents' wedding," replied Billy. "Seems to me she was wearing something funny around her neck then."

Bridgit frowned at the word *funny*, but Willa said, "She was. We have pictures."

Once the pizza was in the oven, Bridgit made Billy and Willa clap in rhythm while she sang her version of London Bridge. "My FAAAIR Lady-O! Oh! Oh! Yeeeeah!" Her hands were still full of oil from patting out dough, and the tea-towel Billy had tied around her just under the armpits was spattered with tomato sauce.

They took a tour of Billy's house and back yard, where they peeked through bushes at the delivery entrance of the supermarket. Bridgit saw an alley cat and tried to entice it into the yard. Willa sat down on the grass. "Uncle Billy, are we hippies?"

He laughed, surprised. "I guess we were, once."

"My friends at school said their parents said we were. What are hippies?"

Billy sat down beside her. "That's a good question. It's just something we were. But — looking back now, it seems like we were all in a — a movie, like. Hippies were — sort of free spirits, I guess. We used to believe in peace and love and free expression. We shared everything. Didn't believe people could own things or own each other." He nibbled on a piece of grass and looked at the sky.

It sounds nice, thought Willa. Even better than *Marjorie Morningstar*. But why did he say 'used to?' "Do they believe in owning their children?"

Billy's head jerked down. He shot a look at her through

narrowed eyes. He probably knows about Dad, she thought.

"C'mon, cat, c'mon, cat!" Bridgit called in a screechy falsetto. Billy's voice was soft. "Don't worry. He'll be back."

"Then why did Mom go to see a lawyer?"

"She just wanted to find out about her rights. Your rights." Some free spirit. "We aren't hippies any more, are we?"

"Half," Billy answered. "Like the pizza. Your dad believed in all those things harder, more. He missed those days more than the rest of us. There are some pictures up there somewhere." He gestured towards the house. "I was the only one who had a camera in those days."

"They never fought or anything, Mom and Dad."

"He loves you and he'll be back. He just went to chase ghosts in the attic."

Bridgit had the alley cat under her arm. "Are there ghosts in your attic?" she asked, her eyes shaped like O's.

"Not in my attic! A skeleton in the odd closet maybe." Billy looked at Willa. "Maybe there are ghosts at that. Anyway, pizza's nearly done. Put the snarly old thing back in the bushes, will you, Bridgit?"

Willa got to her feet and brushed grass clippings off her clothes.

"You become a woman in little bits," said Billy.

Marjorie Morningstar wasn't even a woman yet, and she was seventeen. Willa was only eleven. Could it be that her dad still wasn't all the way grown up?

"Can we see your diamonds?" Bridgit tucked her hand into Billy's and looked up at him with solemn eyes.

"My diamonds?"

"The ones you dig up."

"Oh, the ones I dig up. Those. Well, I traded them in for this mansion. Did you think I kept them in a drawer somewhere?"

Dummy, thought Willa. "Bridgit, he doesn't —"

"Just smell the pizza, ladies!"

Billy set napkins and shakers of spices and cheese in the living room. "We're not allowed to eat in the living room at home," said

Willa.

Bridgit sat cross-legged on the floor beside the coffee table. "This is special, Willie. It's Uncle Billy's first mansion."

"It's a work of art!" cried Billy as he placed the pan on the coffee table in front of them. The cheese had slid off the beetles so that their shiny backs showed. Billy closed the drapes and switched on a gold metal floor lamp with a fringed rose shade. "How about some orange soda?" He disappeared and they heard him on the attic steps, then in the kitchen. When he returned, he held a glittering silver tray. Three wine glasses fizzled with sparkling orange liquid. The heavy drapes and the antique lamp and the silver tray made Willa feel as though she were in an old-fashioned parlour in New York. The studio couch would fit in here.

Bridgit's eyes were shining. She got to her feet and sat down on the chesterfield with her skirt arranged beneath her. Billy handed her a glass, which she took by the stem. "I won't spill," she said in the breathless blonde voice she used when Sybil sat down with her after dinner to have a cigarette. The wine glasses had gold rims. Bridgit took small sips and turned her glass around and around.

Billy served the pizza. "Do you like my finery, ladies? I found it in a box upstairs. Actually, the tray is an heirloom of some kind. One of my mates up at Slave left it behind when he shipped out. If I ever see him again I'll give it back." Billy ravelled up the strings of mozzarella hanging down his beard. "And speaking of heir-looms — did you know you were my namesake, Willa?"

"I'm a namesake?"

"You were almost ready to be born and I waved good-bye to your mom and dad at the airport and hollered, 'Name it after me, will you?' Aren't you glad they didn't call you William? How are the grapes?"

"They don't really taste like anything," said Willa. "They're not bad."

"Whose namesake am I?" asked Bridgit. She drank her soda with her little finger crooked.

"You? Well, maybe Brigitte Bardot's. But I doubt it. I guess you're a — free spirit." He laughed.

"Can I have some more wine please?" Bridgit held out her glass.

"Mom's been gone a long time," said Willa.

Billy poured soda into Bridgit's glass from a bottle wrapped in a towel. "Maybe she decided to take herself out for supper."

Take herself out for supper?

"I know!" yelled Bridgit. "Let's phone Daddy and Sybil in Victoria!"

"Bridgit, it's long distance," said Willa quickly.

"I know how to dial it. I've called Sybil before." The telephone was on a low table by the window. Bridgit got up from the chesterfield, and holding her wine glass in one hand, lowered herself to the floor beside it.

"Bridgit, no!"

"Maybe you should wait for your mother, Bridgit."

Bridgit's fist was on her hip. "I know her number and I want to talk to her. I want to talk to my grandmother and my daddy!" Orange soda slopped over the rim of her glass onto the rug.

"Look, Bridgit, you're spilling."

Bridgit's lower lip curled into a formation Willa always called The Shovel. "I'm sorry, Uncle Billy." Her sobs were soft whimpers, not like the wailing and shrieking she used at home.

Willa stood up. "Bridgit, Sybil has cancer and she's going to die. And Daddy—and she probably won't ever come to our house again."

"I know," said Bridgit. She didn't say it the way she said, "I know" when she didn't really know, sassy and pout-lipped. She just said "I know" through her whimpering, and the tears continued to drop on the lap of her white dress.

"You knew?" Willa felt tears dripping off her chin. Bridgit nodded. "Daddy told me."

"But then why—? Damn, Bridgit! Damn...." Daddy's-not-coming-back-Daddy's-not-coming-back. "Why did you say all that stuff! 'When is Sybil coming? Will she bring her shawl with the scarlet fringes?' Why did you say it?"

"Why didn't Daddy take me along? I asked him. Why didn't he

let me go see her? She had it already when she was here last time. She had it then already. She didn't tell anybody. We're soul-mates. She said."

Billy got up and put the telephone beside her on the floor. "I think you should call her."

"I can't now."

The cheese on the pizza seemed to shrivel before Willa's eyes.

Billy took Bridgit's wine glass and helped her to her feet. She scuffed at the orange stain with her sandal. "Don't worry about the rug. I'm getting a new one next week. Look how rotten this one is!" He lifted the rug at the baseboard and it came up in shreds.

"Another laboratory experiment," suggested Willa as she blotted her eyes with a pizza napkin.

"Do you want to sing "London Bridge"? I have a guitar."

"Not right now."

"Then I'll put the pizza back in the oven and just play for a while."

"You shouldn't swear, Willie."

Willa opened her book. It was hard to concentrate. Fluffy bits swam across the surface of her eyes. Billy took his guitar out of the hall closet and played songs she'd never heard. She reread the part where Marjorie met the song-writer, Noel Airman, for the first time, and a boy named Wally kept giving her cigarettes. Marjorie didn't know how to smoke, but smoked them anyway so Noel would think she was grown up. Bridgit fell asleep on the chesterfield. The orange soda had painted a false smile at the corners of her mouth and tears dried in the corners of her eyes. Willa saw that her red nail polish was chipped from the cat-hunt in the bushes. *She'll probably make phone calls to Sybil's grave.*

Willa parted the drapes at the window and discovered that it was still broad daylight outside. "Can I go up to the attic?"

"Should I show you the pictures?" asked Billy.

"I'd like to look for them myself, if you don't mind me opening up your boxes."

"You'd better take a flashlight with you for the dark corners. There's no electricity up there."

The attic air glowed as she climbed the groaning staircase. The attic was even brighter than it had been before, now that the sun was shining directly through the dirty window. "For someone who shared everything he sure has a lot of stuff," she said to herself. She saw the box the tray had been in, open now, its cardboard flaps gaping at the roof beams.

She squatted and unlocked flaps on other boxes. Paperback novels. Old runners and leather sandals. Magazines: *Macleans* and *Outdoorsman*. Mugs with jokes printed on them. Framed pictures of beaches with palm trees. Record albums — The Mothers of Invention. Collections of empty peanut butter jars.

Bridgit's words haunted the attic. *Why didn't Daddy take me along? Why didn't he let me go see her? We're soul-mates. She said.* Every time Willa felt the lump coming back to her throat and the tears filling the bottoms of her eyes, she'd close a box with a snap of the cardboard lids and pull another towards her.

A flat low box held the photographs. But there were hundreds of them, all in a jumble, and the faces she could make out were the faces of strangers. "I can't look at every single picture in this box, not today." She liked talking out loud to herself in Billy's attic. The sound of her voice helped drown out Bridgit's.

Willa shone the flashlight into the box of photos, then switched it off again. All the people were laughing and had their arms around each other. She was afraid, she realized, afraid that she would see her father looking happier than she'd ever seen him, happier than she was.

Willa leaned back and stretched her legs.

Sybil appeared. She'd been hiding in one of the boxes. She wore real pearls at her neck and in her ears, and was wrapped in a mink coat. She smoked a cigarette in a black holder. Rhinestone bows decorated her shoes. "It smells up here," she said. "It desecrates the silk." A puff of cigarette and she was gone.

Willa reached into the box of photos. There he was, dressed in faded jeans and one of those India cotton shirts she'd seen in a shop in West Edmonton Mall. He was barefoot. His hair was long and wild. Willa recalled the wedding pictures, Sybil with her fox collar and her dyed shoes, Dad in his thongs. They looked alike, everyone said so. But Sybil's face was blank, and she stood off from the wedding party as if they would contaminate her.

My father didn't like his mother much, thought Willa, and she didn't like him.

She thought about the two of them together now — Sybil dying and having to leave her things behind, the things she loved so; her father trying to figure out why he couldn't be a hippie any more, the very thing his mother hated.

Willa felt peaceful. She put the photo back in the box and closed it. "I won't do this today. I'll do it when he comes back."

The sun was setting and the attic grew dark, darker. In the gloom and the dust, Willa sat on an overturned box and waited with the ghosts for the return of her mother.

Stranger on Paradise Bay

Bryce Denby was able to enter the house as silently as though he'd slithered through the mail slot. The latch did not click when he opened the door, nor did it click when he closed it. He did not drop his boots one by one as he removed them, but placed them side by side in the corner of the vestibule that belonged to them. Bryce Denby savoured the few minutes between arriving home and being discovered.

A forty-watt bulb beneath the range-hood lit the kitchen. No messages scribbled on bits of paper. But as he lowered his bassoon case to the floor near the hall entrance, the telephone rang. Bryce held the mouthpiece beneath his chin so that the caller heard nothing more than perfunctory grunts and murmurs. He hated talking on the phone.

Jenny's face appeared and disappeared at the hall doorway. After midnight. What was she doing out of bed?

Bryce hung up the phone and heard the heels of Kate's slippers smacking against the bottoms of her feet. She shuffled out of the dark hallway swathed in lavender chenille. "Who phoned?" she asked through a half-yawn. Her slipper caught on a corner of the bassoon case and it rasped on the tile.

Bryce glared at her over the top of his glass-frames and went to the refrigerator. He stuck his head in. "MacIntosh. Asked me to drive tomorrow. He has to take that millstone of his to the hospital in the morning. Are we out of beer?"

"What's wrong with her?"

"Who?"

"Marilyn MacIntosh."

"I don't know. I think he's having her tongue removed, or she's having a baby or something. We really are out of beer."

"She's not due yet. I hope nothing's wrong. It's right there in front of you." Kate reached around him and took a brown bottle from a cluster of jars.

"Not that swill," he growled. "I'm looking for the Heineken."

"Swill is all. If you don't drink it, why do you buy it?"

"For my red-neck brothers-in-law." Bryce felt Kate's eyes clawing his back as he scanned his collection of beer glasses for one that expressed his disdain.

"And what do you call your relatives?" she asked.

"I call them seldom. And when they're dead and buried they become venerable ancestors." With his tone and posture he closed the conversation, for he had already spirited himself into his favourite chair with his cigarettes and his beer and the latest issue of *Atlantic*. His body followed. Kate stayed in the kitchen to put out Pop-tarts and Cheerios for tomorrow's breakfast. Bryce heard the cereal box tip over, the fripple of hundreds of toasty-O's hitting the floor. "Damn!" he breathed. Sugary dust all over the kitchen.

"Damn!" said Kate.

Kate never swore. "Trouble in paradise," Bryce mumbled, and went to the stereo. He pulled out his new Wagner recordings. The hand vacuum cleaner whined in the kitchen.

Kate settled into her rocking-chair across from his contoured recliner. Bryce stood with his back to her, picking at flecks of lint and hair on the record surface. How did lint and hair manage to infiltrate a record sleeve the moment it was open? Unless....

"How did it go tonight?" Kate asked.

"Did you play these when I was gone?"

"Oh sure. As soon as you leave the house, Jenny and Jason and I sneak into your collection and go wild with your Schütz and Mahler."

"You could do worse."

"How did it go tonight?" She was impatient.

"I'm glad you came yesterday. We were better yesterday. *They* were, My timing was impeccable, of course. Want some cognac?"

She shook her head. The music burst into the room and Kate caught Bryce's hand as he walked past her chair.

Bryce stared down at the top of her head, at the straight parting down the centre. Strands of grey radiated from it and then mixed with walnut-brown curls. When he turned the volume lower, he heard the wind rising outside.

In his chair, he lit a Cameo and poured beer into the Pilsner glass. The foam hissed.

"Jen was attacked in school today," said Kate.

Ah. So that's why Kate damned the Cheerios. "What do you mean 'attacked'? Morally, ethically, what?"

"Physically, damn it! By a pack of grade nines."

An old bitterness seeped into the room with the wind. "This place will get her, too, won't it? They'll get her."

"Do you want to hear about it or do you think ranting to the strains of *Götterdämmerung* will heal your daughter?" Kate leaned forward and fumbled with the cigarette package. Bryce seized it from her and handed her a smoke. He lit it. "She was hysterical when she got home from school, but I think it went something like this: she was on her way to French, by herself — I think she was late for some reason or other —"

"Why was she late?"

"— and she saw four boys in front of her. She says she was scared because they were looking at her and laughing, but she couldn't really avoid them. So she was going to walk around them, and one boy put her arm around her chest and another boy moved up against her."

"She should have kneed him. Animals. What do we have to do,

slick her up with bear grease before sending her off to school every morning?"

"She should have kneed him? Jenny? Anyway, they just sort of hassled her, 'handed her around,' she said, until they saw a teacher coming, and then they took off." Kate put her head back against the wooden head-rest of the rocker and took a long breath. Bryce's fingers carved Wagnerian rhythms in the plush arms of his chair. They sat without speaking for some minutes. Then Kate added, "She started crying after that, and says she felt humiliated because a teacher saw her crying and she couldn't explain to him what was wrong."

Bryce's fingers stopped. "Did she use the word 'humiliated'?"

"Yes."

The fingers danced again. Bryce took a long draught of his beer.

Kate continued. "She didn't tell anyone in school. The teacher just led her to the girls' washroom, and she stayed there until last bell and came home."

"They got away with it."

"She said they were all puny."

"That's all we've got in this ghetto, puny grade-niners," Bryce sneered. "This entire place has the mentality of fourteen-year-olds. We should have stayed in St. Cloud." He strode to the stereo and turned it louder, as though the beat of the music would flog the assailants for their crime.

Bryce looked at his wife, dark and silhouetted against the window and the light from the boulevard. He saw the taut line of her jaw and the hard set of her shoulders. He wanted to say that Jennifer had seemed normal at supper that evening, but he knew he had not paid much attention, as usual. He'd been immersed in his score through the entire meal, and hadn't sensed her distress. And he was afraid that Kate might say all this to him, here, tonight, finally. He paced between the chair and the window. "Children should be arranged behind glass windows like whores in Amsterdam, and when they're eighteen, parents could go and pick one out that they like and take him home for dinner and cigars."

Kate rose and stared out the window, arms folded under her

breasts. "It probably won't be her last experience like this. I've called Mrs. Duncan. We're to see her at four o'clock tomorrow. Can you come home early?"

Bryce went to the large square window and stood with her, looking out. Paradise Bay. Choose from a variety of designs: Tudor, Elizabethan, Mojave, Palm Beach. People had planted trees. Young lawyers and teachers and civil servants had waved to one another in their driveways. Babies had babbled on the new sod. Fences went up, swimming pools went in. Then, new schools without windows rose at the outskirts. The children grew. '64 convertibles, colourless because of rust and dents, cruised the bay without their mufflers. Gashes appeared in garage doors, holes in fences. Trick-or-treaters had their candy stolen by bullies dressed like clowns. Drugs and knives haunted the schools. People didn't wave to each other any more. Skunks nested under patios.

Bryce felt Kate's hand squeezing his upper arm. "Look at MacIntosh out there jogging. I guess Marilyn is all right. At midnight, in this wind, he's jogging." She smiled up at Bryce. "You know, he's got a nice physique. Flat stomach." She thumped his paunch.

He brushed past her to his worn, cupped chair. After a deep sigh, he said, "I'll go down and talk to her. To Jenny."

"Let her sleep." Kate spoke into the glass in front of her. "We did pick them out from a window, didn't we, in a way?" She went to the kitchen with the empty beer bottle.

He couldn't give her children. When they'd found out seventeen years ago, Bryce had tormented Kate with prolonged silences, followed by maniacal onslaughts of eunuch jokes. Bryce always told their friends he'd stolen Kate from the tympanist, who was hairy and ate steak every day. Bryce had hardly ever dated women. He couldn't believe his luck in snatching Kate away from a hairy tympanist. He told her to go back to him.

Kate had finally packed a bag and left the house. When she'd returned a week later, Bryce had slumped to the door to greet her, slovenly and miserable, and they began to speak about adopting. Bryce thought about MacIntosh, jogging, copulating, fathering babies, fulfilling the maternal desires of his sausagey, tongue-wagging wife. That slob.

Kate called out, "This Saturday is Jason's first morning practice. Brewster phoned earlier to remind us. He's supposed to be there at seven." Bryce heard her rummaging in the freezer. "I know that's a little early for you, but you promised to be there the first time." The Wagner swelled again and Bryce conducted from his chair, pulling and releasing the strains of music with imaginary strings as though flying a kite. He should have been a conductor, a celibate symphony conductor. It would have been easier to be a celibate conductor than a celibate second-rate bassoonist-lawyer.

When he noticed Kate watching him from the doorway, he said, "Eight is too young to be playing a high-pressure sport. He should be taking piano lessons instead of consorting with ham-fisted dolts." But they'd already spent many desperate months at the piano with their young son, struggling with his awkward fingers while he struggled with deciphering notes. Hockey was his desire and finally they had agreed to the seven A.M. workouts. And both Kate and Bryce wondered if things would have been different had their children been born to them.

"Do you think we should try him on another instrument?" Kate said.

"How about drums?" Maybe he'd become a world-class tympanist.

"Well, I'm off to bed. Oh, did you have lunch with Bill today?"

Bryce lowered his magazine. His voice was vinegary. "We went to that new place downtown. It turned out to be one of those urban cowboy joints — you know, fake beams and waitresses in buckskin. Very embarrassing. They put an olive in my whisky and coke."

"Black or green? I'll put your bassoon away." Kate left the room, clenching her toes so that her slippers didn't slap against the bottoms of her feet.

Bryce held the beer glass level with his eyes and examined the streetlight through its thickness, turning it to watch the shape of the light change and distort with the flaws in the glass. *I should talk to Jenny.* He thought about her being 'handed around' by the circle of boys. The music faded away. He began it again, and wished that he could look through the window and see the stars.

The wind was as strong the next afternoon, only more blustery, · swaggering and strutting along the city streets like the spirit of an Othello. Rain was in the air, a vapour flung about without ever reaching the ground, although it spattered against the car windows every so often, making slender needles of wet on the glass. At a red light at the intersection near the school, Kate and Bryce's car rocked as a sudden gust caught it broadside.

"Christ, it's blowing bunnies out there!" It was a phrase Bryce used with his daughter in stormy weather. When she was six she'd found a baby cottontail pressed against the side of the garage during a summer storm. She'd brought it into the house for warmth and childish protection. When Bryce advised her to let it go, Jen had cried, fearing that the bunny would be blown away by the wind. Though Jen was not in the car now, Bryce felt her presence there, riding in the back seat. "Wind makes people irritable, Kate. It is not a day for principals and paradisians to be discussing puberty."

"Too many p's."

"Look at that god-awful building. Reminds me of the rest home your Uncle Rufus the Unreal frequented for many years before he fell off his tractor and got cured by an eccentric deep-tiller."

"I don't know. It's not so bad when jocks are tossing basketballs through those hoops."

"Ah! Something I've obviously missed."

The corridors were nearly empty. Kate and Bryce passed a noisy bunch of hangers-on in the lobby, who were making a variety of animal-like sounds. "Like gibbons descending trees after the tigers have left," Bryce whispered. Inside the quieter main hallway, a mingled smell of leather and Lysol cloyed at his nose, while stragglers slammed lockers shut in a chorus of defiance. He saw Kate suppressing a smile as young girls in tired, blotchy make-up slipped along the halls, great floppy notebooks and gaudy binders tucked underneath their arms. In the absence of the crowd they slouched like old women.

Kate and Bryce walked along the hall towards the administrative offices. She was excited by the atmosphere of the high school. At first Bryce attempted to maintain his irreverent banter just below earshot of the young people in the hallway, but he'd withered in the peaceful coos and clucks of reminiscence uttered by Kate at his side, and withdrew into the shelter of her definition. It was always that way.

He'd first seen Kate at the tympanist's house on a hot July afternoon. In those days, Bryce drove from St. Cloud, where he had a partnership in a small firm, to the city for rehearsals. He'd gone to the tympanist's to deal on a Ford, and there'd been Kate, sunning herself in the back yard, wearing a white bathing suit and lying on a lavender beach towel on the brilliant green grass. Bryce fell in love with the colours, and then her thick brown hair, and then her serenity. They kept meeting at concerts. One evening the brutish boyfriend faded away completely. Kate and Bryce got married and lived in St. Cloud until they began to plan their family. Through thick and thin, she maintained definition.

Bryce recognized something in the hallway. He stopped. A bronze plaque on the wall commemorated the untimely deaths of fifteen or twenty students of the Raymond Kosleck High School. Most of them were boys. Bryce recalled a similar tribute in his school. It had only one name on it when he attended, but then the town was small and the school new. Bryce couldn't remember the name, but he'd known the boy a little, because the boy had owned a motorcycle. Motorcycles were scarce in Bryce's home-town in those days, but this boy had owned one and had ridden it to school. Bryce envied his popularity. He had few friends, but found himself lingering at the edge of other friendships. Bryce never gawked at the bike with the others. He secretly longed to get on the shiny black motorcycle and drive recklessly through all the streets of town. The boy had collided with a car one day, landing on a coarse gravel shoulder and leaving his admirers to dream about his pain and the gleaming wreckage.

When Bryce finally looked away from the bronze plaque, he was startled to see a face — half of a face — near him, along the vertical edge of a locker door. The young man was watching him with one cold eye. The part of the face Bryce could see, though shadowed, was smooth, unblemished. Short, clean dark hair. The nostril was slightly flared, as though the smells in the corridor were too pungent. The tension in the arch of his jaw, the curve of his lip, struck Bryce with a jolt of recognition. It was his own reflection in a darkened window.

The boy looked away and slammed the locker door. After a twist of the combination dial, he turned his back on Bryce and walked down the hallway. He held his head high and did not look from side to side as he went. Bryce watched him until he turned into the library at the far end of the wing.

It could have been his son, so alike were they. Again he thought of the crowd of boys around the black motorcycle, the one boy at the edge.... He turned and strode in his soft-soled shoes towards the serene swaying figure of Kate, ahead of him in the hallway.

Vice-principal Webber, standing in for an absent *Ms.* Duncan, was also the guidance counsellor at the school. Bryce remained suspicious, he had little regard for title, but held forth on his suburban ghetto theme only half-heartedly. He spent most of the thirty minutes browsing through Principal Duncan's library. Kate and Webber exchanged anxieties.

...distressed...thoroughly detestable...afraid to come back... most unfortunate...dealt with severely...hard to adjust....

Horny pimple-faced satyrs, chanted a chorus in Bryce's mind. The voices fused, and though he paged through a copy of *Bleak House*, he remembered the face of the boy, the face partially hidden by the locker door. He pictured Jennifer's face, Jason's face, on that rigid body, their freckles beneath that cold eye....

He saw that Kate was sitting just as she always did with school authorities, or doctors, or the head of Jen's music academy — leaning forward in her chair, her back straight, one side of her body relaxed, open, the other side flexed and ascendant. She was like a marble statue. The book tipped forward onto Bryce's chest as he looked past Kate to the window. Rain streamed diagonally across the pane.

Mr. Webber leaned back in his chair and pressed a button. The fluorescent light on the ceiling flickered. Bryce's hand went to his brow and he frowned at the carpet.

"Energy," said Webber, and he pointed to the ceiling with a long black pen. He opened a file on the desk. "Anyway, Mrs. Denby, Jennifer is doing well in her academics. Seems to excel in the arts. She plays the flute, I believe? Yes, a real flair there." He muttered a few more comments about "slight-problem-with-geometry-nothing-serious-you-understand" and Bryce was just about to slide the book back into its place on the shelf, to indicate the end of the meeting, when he heard, "So, if she could just work on this one little flaw, I'm sure she'll make out all right in the future."

In the future meant he intended to end the conference there. But, "'Flaw?'"

Webber leaned onto his desk in a semblance of calm, but the sudden tension in the room blistered up in creases along the upper arm of his suit jacket. "Perhaps *flaw* is too bleak a word. But it's not the least bit unusual for young girls who are just beginning to notice their bodies to get a little carried away sometimes."

"Are you saying our daughter is a floozy?" Bryce moved forward, legs apart like a gun-slinger. The straight line of Webber's mouth expanded into a humorless smile. "Of course not, Mr. Denby. She's not unlike the other girls here, other girls her age, a bit."

"I get the picture," said Bryce. He saw Kate look at him. She was biting the inside of her bottom lip, which meant she was afraid Bryce was about to go out of control. But he could think of nothing to say. He was the stranger on Paradise Bay. Its perils were only rituals after all.

"You've taken us by surprise, Mr. Webber," said Kate. "Jennifer's never struck us as being a — a vivacious type of girl. We think we know her pretty well...."

"We don't know her, Kate," said Bryce, *melodramatically*, Kate would say later.

The vice-principal's eyebrows lifted. Bryce wanted to laugh.

"I'm afraid I've been a bit tactless here," said Webber. "But please don't discount your daughter's — ah — femininity in this matter." He shuffled his feet under his chair. The fluorescent light began to buzz.

The walk back along the corridor was brisk. Outside in the wind and rain Kate's shoes slapped on the wet concrete.

As Bryce hunched over the car door with the key, he saw the boy from the locker walking alone across the flat, stormy campus. The wind snatched some papers from the boy's armful of home-work, threw them down onto the grass, then flipped them up and away again just as he was about to retrieve them. Bryce jerked in the direction of the papers; the impulse was as automatic as if the papers had been his. The boy noticed someone was watching, and with a petulant gesture, gave up the chase.

It was not an invisible Jennifer riding in the back seat now, but a nameless child-woman. Neither Kate nor Bryce spoke for a long time during the ride home, a ride made as arduous by rush-hour traffic and barricaded street lanes as the ascent of a steep cliff. Home, though not far from the school, seemed difficult to get to.

"Do you think she — flirts?" said Bryce at last.

"I thought she had a crush on her flute teacher," said Kate.

"That's not what I'm paying him for."

"Did you think turning your daughter into a flautist would render her sexless?"

"Why not? It worked for her bassoonist-father." Kate boxed him in the ear. "Well, I didn't expect flute lessons to change her into a nymphomaniac."

"They haven't. Webber is sexist. Couldn't you tell? Do you really think Jen asked to be abused by those creeps?"

I don't know how to protect her from it all, thought Bryce. Kate can do it, she must do it. I can't.

Kate slid down a little in her seat, shrugged her shoulders to loosen them, and closed her eyes.

Bryce drummed the steering wheel with his fingers as they waited for the light to change. " 'Ah — please don't discount your daughter's — ah — femininity in this matter.' "

Kate reached for Bryce's dancing fingers and squeezed them.

"Talk to her. She has to hear from a man that she hasn't been soiled."

Supper was late. Bryce brooded throughout the meal and ate slowly. Jason played soundless war games in his plate, Jennifer kept her eyes lowered and picked at her food, while Kate murmured reminders about table manners and nutrition.

Jason spoke at last into his dish of Rocky-Road ice cream. "I have a game next Saturday afternoon." He paused. "Will you come?" He glanced at his father's butter-knife. Bryce waited for Jason's eyes to rise in expectation to meet his. But Jason's eyes slid across the table and latched onto Kate's.

"You haven't even learned to walk on your skates and already you've got a game scheduled?" said Bryce.

"Posilutely," answered Jason, making a catapult of his teaspoon.

"Haven't I told you not to play with your food? And not to use that idiotic lingo?"

"Absotively."

Bryce took a long, slow sip of coffee while looking over the rim at his son. "I'll be there." Kate and Jennifer stared at him.

"One-thirty." This time Jason spoke directly to Bryce.

Bryce looked at Kate. "Can you take Jennifer to her lesson next Saturday?"

Jennifer jumped up with her dishes in her hands and blurted out, "I'm quitting flute lessons." She turned and went to the kitchen sink. Her knife and fork clattered to the floor.

The wind died during the long evening. Bryce stepped out onto the back porch every half-hour or so to see if the clouds had thinned out. Kate had taken asylum in her workroom — she didn't like people calling it a *studio* — where she was preparing preliminary sketches for some watercolours of pondscapes. Bryce wanted to go and tell her when he was finally able to make out Polaris in the northern sky. But her contentment when she was painting irritated him, even though she never seemed to be aggravated by interruptions. The children had also shut themselves in their rooms. In the absence of the wind, the atmosphere was a vacuum, airless and still. Bryce listened for the sound of Jennifer's flute. He sat in his chair between prowls until he realized that he might dispel the vacuum with his own music, and put *Tristan and Isolde* on the stereo.

Shortly after ten he went to the kitchen and opened the cupboard doors and stared at the rows of mugs and glasses. Kate came in and laid out the next day's breakfast by the dim light over the stove. Bryce remained frozen at the open cupboard.

"I bought the Heineken this morning," she said.

"Mm."

"Have you talked to Jen?"

"I don't know what to say."

"They're not like those bloody mugs of yours, Bryce. We can't just bring them home and then fill them up with — with *ourselves*. Just talk to her about anything. Don't even mention all those things that hurt so much. Forget the puny grade-niners, forget her wanting to quit her music lessons, forget Paradise Bay. Ask her what she wants for Christmas." Kate pressed against his back and put her arms around his waist.

"I saw someone I knew today, at the school, someone I knew well. He was familiar to me right away, but it only occurred to me much later that I knew him." Bryce took a glass from the shelf at last and closed the doors. "I need them to kill him off, at least, part of him. It's a very refined distillation process." The beer trickled from the bottle into a rising bed of foam in the glass.

Bryce took his ale, and Kate her cognac, in a teacup as a joke, into the back yard, though it was a cold night. Kate hummed along with the Wagner they could hear through the partially opened Tudor window. MacIntosh panted in the alley and then slammed his back door.

"You can't see the stars from here," fretted Bryce. "I've always wanted to see Andromeda and Cassiopeia and the Pleiades and all those fine women up there. Especially the Pleiades." He pitched his spent cigarette into the grass. "Did you know that Zeus tossed the seven of them up there to help them escape from the hunter Orion? One's disappeared, though. Some say she hid herself in shame for having married a mortal." He caught the back of Kate's neck with his cupped hand. "Poor little lost Pleiad. She was a nymph, too, you know."

"Do you think that skunk's moved out from under the porch? I'm always afraid of meeting him out here after dark."

"Me big hunter Orion. Me get big gun."

The record ended. Kate, slipperless tonight, felt chilled and went inside. The comfortable chair, the music, the streetlight moon retreated as the edge of the city reposed, windless and damp. "Poor little lost Pleiad," said Bryce. He clutched the beer glass to his chest and waited for the sound of the flute to mingle with the clear night air.

Lipstick the Colour of Apples

Lucille sat on her bed and painted her mouth with lipstick the colour of apples. She applied it to each lip with a stiff, deliberate motion, beginning at one corner of her mouth and ending at the other, leaving a shapeless blot. Her face, otherwise colourless and taut, looked like an unfinished portrait. She snapped the lipstick tube closed and looked at her room-mate at the desk near the window. "Two Bibles, now? You must be religious."

Lily said nothing, but switched on her wall lamp and whispered verses to herself.

"A beautiful sunset on the other side, and we sit here in the dark staring at the stone wall." Lucille flexed her ankles. "Let's ask for a different room. I want to see the river." She watched Lily's finger embroider the thin pages in front of her. "We could watch the rich men in their boats."

Lily's finger stopped. "Ha! Boats? Go and watch sometime. They'd be shipwrecked, like that!" She smacked her hands together.

"Well, at least it would be something to see."

"It's too big and full. Scary, that's what I say. We should be thinking about the poor sick people in there." Lily nodded towards the window.

A large hospital of grey rock loomed just outside their small room. "Tyndall stone," Lucille had heard the nurse say to a new patient just that morning, like a tour guide. "It's sort of rare — you find it only in this one certain place just like you find jade in the Fraser River. That makes it special, don't you think?" The new patient, not knowing or having forgotten jade, the Fraser River, or not caring, remained mute like the stone itself. And poised between a swollen river that was chaotic with broken ice and swift water, and that grey stone expanse of hospital, the new wooden psychiatric ward of the Saint Mary Health Centre seemed to hover between tumult and tyndall. The white trim around the shatterproof windows and the handrails leading up to the front door looked cheerful on the outside, but inside became unrelenting. Except for the maple-veneered furnishing in the wards and the common rooms, all was white, even the slack daisies at patients' bedsides. In the dining rooms, thick chains connected steel bottle-openers to the wall. With the bottle-openers you could uncap bottles, or, with the other end, cut a neat triangular gash into a tin of orange juice. The chains were bolted to the walls.

Lucille stood up. "We are having a party tonight. You come."

"Why do you always put that lipstick on? Twenty times a day you paint your mouth, and in a few minutes it's all chewed away."

Lucille went to the closet and took out a pair of red sandals. She tossed her black felt slippers into a corner and put on the red shoes. When she straightened up her cheeks were pink. Her heels clicked on the tile floor. She heard voices murmuring in the common room next to the kitchen, where a few visitors spoke to wives, mothers, sisters, daughters. Attendants in white coats revolved through the passageways around the ward and looked for signs of danger. In an urn in the hallway, pussy willows caught the redness of the sun and glowed with a hundred flames.

Lucille wandered into the dining room and stopped to run her fingertip along the edge of the pointy end of the bottle-opener. She looked at the chain joining it with the wall.

Why had they tied her hands? When her head cleared and she

could see and feel again, she found she was tied by her wrists to her bedposts. They had used white package twine from the drawer in the kitchen where they kept scotch tape and scissors and rubber jar rings. She remembered putting on her lipstick and asking if she could go to the river, and they had said no. They never said why and they always said no. She remembered a child's voice asking, "Why do you want to go to the river, Nana?" And she was about to answer, and then.... And then what? When her head cleared, she found her hands tied. Her own daughter had tied her to the bed because she had asked to go to the river. She felt like a moth pinned to a board.

Lucille found the window facing the river and watched the sun moving down and the river moving towards and away from the wooden building.

She returned to the doorway of her room. Lily still mouthed her Bible verses. "We're having a party tonight," she repeated. "It's arranged. It will be starting soon. Forget your Bible and come, Lily."

Lily looked at Lucille's lips glowing in the doorway. "What do you mean, a party?" She plucked at her own brown double-knit slacks. "I don't see any frilly dresses."

"The men are coming and we are going to move the furniture, dance, and have cigarettes." Lucille began to rock her shoulders in rhythm and snap her fingers.

"Cigarettes? I've never seen you smoke. Why do you need cigarettes?"

"What's a party without cigarettes? You don't know much about parties." Lucille sat on her bed again and opened her lipstick tube. "Haven't you ever been to one?"

The Gideon Bible thumped closed. "In Russia I went to lots of parties when I was a young girl. And do you know what I did there, Miss Party-Smarty? I played the guitar while everyone danced. That's what I know about parties. The men smoked and the ladies wore fancy dresses."

Lucille stared for a moment at Lily's silhouette against the lamplight, then laughed in a high, thin voice. "Have you talked to your therapist about this? She'd love to hear it."

"We talk only about my Sarah."

"Everyone has a Sarah. Or was one."

"But…we must still obey the Lord. That is the hardest by far."

Lily looked out the window. "Don't your children visit you, Lucille?"

"Who wants a crazy woman?"

A silence followed but Lucille did not care for it. "So if you were such a party-girl, when did you get religious, I'd like to know?"

"I never danced. I never even looked. I just played."

"Didn't you dance at your wedding? Didn't you twirl around in a white satin gown?"

"I had a white satin dress. When my son was a little boy I cut it up and made Sunday blouses for him. He had a white cap and a white sweater I knit from real wool. He was the nicest looking at church on Sundays, and he kept clean. He kept so nice and clean. I have a picture of him standing on a milking stool in the barn."

This was the most Lucille had heard Lily say. Lucille had arrived here first, much earlier than Lily. Poor thing, she thought. And what had she kept for herself? "You cut up your wedding gown?"

"I didn't need it any more."

"My husband left me six months after we got married. I was pregnant with my daughter. He came home a few years later to die. That's all my daughter ever knew of her father. A stranger dying in our house. I never got married again, but I still have my wedding dress."

"What do you mean, you never got married again? You're still alive, aren't you? Maybe you'll find a nice bachelor at the party tonight and you can be a bride again."

"That would be really crazy." Lucille laughed through her nose as she applied more lipstick. Her feet tapped to a beat inside her head. "And where's your guitar now? You could play for us tonight. And not look."

"Where is this party? Not outside my door, I hope."

"In the lounge that faces the river. It's the nicest one. And Marlon is bringing us ginger ale, for a change, with ice."

"Marlon?"

"Marlon Brando," replied Lucille. "You don't know who Marlon Brando is, do you?" She stopped squirming. "He was my favourite, not so very long ago. He had—a mouth—he wasn't the other girls' favourite though—they didn't like that sweaty T-shirt at all, but—he's in the Old Testament, the Book of Deuteronomy, chapter five, verses four to thirty-three." Lucille snapped the tube shut. "And you thought I didn't know anything about religion." She sat down on the bed to brush her hair. "Didn't you ever have a favourite? Billy Graham, or the Mormon Tabernacle Choir or something?"

Lily waved her hand to brush the question away.

"That old man who comes to see you? With the cane and the pimple under his eye?" Lucille winked with one eye at Lily.

"It doesn't make any difference."

"No. You're here. He didn't help much, did he? He never sent you an autographed eight-by-ten in the mail." Lucille's hairbrush clattered into the drawer of her night-table.

She could have easily gotten away, it was just white package twine. But she had no strength to pull herself free of the white strings. She felt thin and stick-like in her nightgown, as though her body were missing the fullness it used to have. She couldn't even pull at the white strings. The next day they brought her here. She didn't belong here. They're the ones who had tied her wrists to the bedposts. She hadn't tied herself to the bedposts. Had she?

"Well, you're here, too, aren't you?" Lily said. She turned towards the window and watched the lights going on in the stone building.

"You know why we're having a party?" asked Lucille. "It's for that young girl who came in last—last—whenever. You know, she's only sixteen, I found out. Did you see her long hair? We both had hair like that once, didn't we? My grandchild has long hair like that. Did your Sarah have long hair?"

Lily did not answer.

Lucille stared into a space at the foot of Lily's bed and sucked on her lips. "She closed her father's garage door and ran the car engine. In the garage. With her poodle." Lucille stood, placed her index finger on the middle of her head and pirouetted through the door.

"How do you know that?" shouted Lily. "No one would tell you that!"

Lights flashed on in the wooden building on the riverbank. The common room had emptied, although men and women drifted in now and then to look in the refrigerator. They were not thirsty or hungry, but liked seeing the colours of the fruit juices stored like jewels in a cool white vault. Most of the patients were in their rooms. Some played shuffleboard in the rec room, as though passing time on a cruise ship during bad weather.

In the west lounge, Lucille turned the radio dial back and forth, and the radio spat out sounds in fits of melodies and static interference. The volume rose and fell, echoed from blank walls. The dial came to rest at a blare of 'forties band tunes.

Lucille stood at the picture window and gnawed on her bottom lip while she watched the river below. An ice floe, flung up against someone's boathouse a little downstream, dissolved in the swirling water.

Finding her wrists tied to the bedposts, she didn't cry out or try to move. She lay there, as still as a stone, until they came and untied the knots. Why? She remembered turning to her granddaughter to answer, and then.... And then what? She had to get to the river.

Lucille swayed to the music. When she turned, Martin, the orderly, clean and smooth as a vinyl doll, was sitting on the arm of a maple-coloured sofa. "Ah, Marlon! Let's dance. Help me move this table." Lucille moved towards the coffee-table but Martin had picked it up and set it against the wall before she was there.

Lucille began a ragged foxtrot. "I wanted Doris to come. You know, from the end of the hall? But she's gone. She went home this morning. It's too bad she'll miss the party. Maybe if I'd told her about it before she left. Although she might be back. Not likely so soon, though. She won't get to meet that girl. Too bad. Though she might be back before the girl leaves." Lucille stopped to adjust a strap on her sandal before she continued dancing and talking. Her voice rose above the trombones and saxophones. "Lily won't come. She's just obsessed with that crucifixion. She has no sense of romance, Marlon." Lucille threw back her head and laughed.

When the music ended, Martin offered to recruit more revellers from the ward.

"Oh, can the girl come down, Marlon? The pretty girl? Then we'll get people out, you listen to me." She patted the pocket of her cardigan. "Tell her I have something for her. And tell her she'll feel better if she comes to the party." Martin left and Lucille continued dancing.

Men wearing robes with large buttons wandered into the lounge in slippers. One of the men saw Lucille dancing at the window and cheered before he sat down to watch her. Two women from the room next to Lucille's and Lily's came to the party wearing their best pant-suits, with their hair brushed back and extra rouge on their cheeks. They danced with each other, fumbling at harmonizing their steps. What with the nervous giggles and the music, a semblance of gaiety soon emerged from the west lounge. Lucille passed the cigarettes around with the flair of a bon vivant. Everyone took one, but few of the guests smoked them. A small man, enchanted by Lucille's red shoes, jumped up from his chair. He checked all his buttons with bony fingers and invited her to waltz with him. Lucille's laughter pierced the closed doors along the halls as she and her partner shuffled about the dance floor.

Martin came in with a tray. "Refreshments!" cried Lucille. She handed out the white styrofoam cups of ginger ale. "We need a toast!" Someone turned down the radio and Lucille raised her cup unsteadily above her head. A drop of liquid spilled over the top and down the transparent skin of her hand and down her wrist. "To — to — Marlon, the girl...?"

"Rachel," he answered.

When the styrofoam cups touched, the squeaks sent tremors

through thin-boned arms.

"Rachel," Lucille repeated. "Is she coming? Turn up the music. No, wait. Let's find another station. She probably doesn't like that crap. That won't get her down here." Lucille went to the radio and twirled the knobs. As the volume rose again, the merry-makers froze, waiting to be propelled into the next moment of their celebration. "Well, come on!" Lucille called. "This is a party. Should I teach you how to do it right? Come on, Marlon. We'll show these old tits!" Lucille waved her arms and bounced on her red sandals. Her grey hair floated about her face like feathers.

A few more patients came to the entrance of the lounge. A white nurse from the shadows beyond the party-room summoned Martin as cries rose above the festivity in the west lounge. Everyone began to dance. Lucille shouted instructions, but stopped in mid-sentence when she saw a white-clad figure in the semi-darkness beyond the doorway. "Rachel."

The girl held a pillow under her arm, a sprig of pussy willow in her hand. Her face was like a stone.

Lucille rushed to her. "Come in, dear." Rachel did not acknowledge the greeting. She brushed past Lucille, skirted the dancers and went by the window, stopping in front of a rocking chair at the far wall. She curled up in the chair and crushed the pillow to her body like a teddy bear. Lucille followed her and crouched at her side. "Here. Here, I have something for you." Lucille reached into her pocket. The girl lowered one foot to the floor and jerked the chair around, away from Lucille. She stared at the bare wall, guarding her self-absorption. Lucille pulled her hand out of her pocket and thrust her closed fist under Rachel's nose. When she opened her palm the lipstick case glittered. "You must keep yourself nice, even here," Lucille said, her face close to Rachel's ear. "Don't let yourself end up like them. Keep yourself pretty, Rachel. Or all you'll get is an old man with a pimple under his eye. You may not believe that now." As Lucille's hand slid up the back of the chair, her fingertips encountered a cobwebby softness. She began to stroke the young girl's hair, and then to fondle it. Rachel did not take the lipstick, so Lucille pressed it into her cold, clenched hand. Its coldness reminded Lucille of the pieces of ice in the river that rushed past the window of the west lounge.

All she had wanted was to go there. They always said no. She had nothing. They'd sold her house and they used her things as though they owned them. All she had left was her wedding gown. They didn't dare touch it. They didn't want to touch it. And when they'd untied the knots, she'd noticed she was still wearing her wool slippers. The bottoms were soiled and crusted, as if she had walked in mud.

A Coca-Cola commercial interrupted the music. The dancers sat down to rest and drank more ginger ale; Lucille passed around more cigarettes.

Should she cry out now? Not yet....

It was in that shift from forgetful frivolity to sudden exhaustion that one man, overtaken by his anxiety, decided to leave the party. He tripped on a corner of his robe as he rose from the sofa, and fell with a sharp gasp. Although he was a small man, the fall had been heavy and he didn't seem to want to get up again. When the music began, he stayed on his knees with his eyes closed and his arms wrapped around his chest. Tears flowed down his cheeks and along his jaw.

At first no one noticed the next arrival. Clad in a yellowed nightgown flaccid from obsessive laundering and the restlessness of many bad nights, she stood like a statue in the doorway. The elastic cut into her skin at her wrists. She held a Gideon Bible against her shoulder, and in the other hand, held aloft high above her head, was the gleaming bottle-opener from the ward kitchen, clutched like a crucifix. The chain hung along her rigid arm.

Lucille first sensed her presence, although her back was to the door, as she poured ginger ale into a cup for Rachel. She straightened and turned. "Lily."

"Who brought you out of the land of Egypt? Out of the house of

bondage? You shall have no other gods before...before Him...."
The revellers stood up. All eyes focused on the relic in Lily's out-
stretched hand. The music roared, but Lily's voice knifed through
it. "...and you shall not make for yourself a graven image...."

"Lily!" What would Rachel think? Lucille stepped forward to
shoo away the demons that possessed Lily.

"...or any likeness of anything that is in heaven above, or that is
in the earth beneath, or that is in the water under the earth.... You
shall not bow down! The Lord your God has commanded you! He is
a jealous God...live long in the land you possess...." The words
ceased.

Although she did not change her pose, Lily seemed to sag, to
wither like a plucked leaf. Martin came up behind her. His face
registered no reaction, not surprise, alarm, nor amusement, when
he saw the shiny instrument in Lily's hand. He maintained his
passive expression, as if he were accustomed to his charges
wrenching chains out of the wall. He brought Lily's hand down
with a strong, clinical motion. The bottle-opener clinked as it hit
the floor, the chain rattled. Martin picked them up. Lily gazed
across the room at the girl. With Martin's firm hand on her arm,
she turned. Lucille stared after them, watching the ebb of Lily's
brief vigour, watching her being led away from the party, back to a
room facing the hospital wall.

Lucille turned to Rachel now, and as she did so, heard Lily
whispering to Martin. "She can use my guitar, but she shouldn't
watch." The girl rocked in her chair, her body twisted toward the
wall. She was no longer a lonely figure against the blank white wall.
Her companion was a stick-figure, drawn with a school-girl
tidiness in bright red outlines, a stick-girl with long, thick red hair
and a little stick-dog at her side. Lucille bore down on Rachel and
snatched the lipstick away. "No — you —!" Lucille sputtered. The
flattened cake of red was now almost gone. Rachel's hair had fallen
across one side of her face. She looked up at Lucille with fierce eyes.
Tears flowed down pale cheeks that were still freckled like a child's.
"They don't let you keep anything here, either," said Lucille.

Darkness had overtaken the river. Fragments of ice gleamed

here and there as they passed among shadows of trees. Lucille stood
by the window. "The river is so high. But don't worry. This place is
built on a hill. The water would never reach it." She looked at
Rachel still curled in the chair, her nightgown concealing the shape
of her body. "You'll make a lovely bride," said Lucille. Then she
followed the other patients as they trickled out into the hallway,
leaving the girl alone with the drumbeats from the radio still
pumping into the room.

With her cardigan wrapped around her, Lucille walked along
the corridors, avoiding windows and open doors.

Should she cry out now? Not yet....

She snapped off a twig of pussy willow as she passed the urn.
Her own feet stepped out in front of her, one after the other.

Someone called, "Are you lost, Lucy?" She went to her room.

Lily was in bed when Lucille came in. Lucille could see her thin
legs and arms outlined in the blue woolen blanket. Sedated, Lucille
thought. As Lucille swam in the folds of her nightgown, she heard
Lily whispering. Praying, thought Lucille. But then Lily spoke
aloud, her voice firm: "There is no Marlon Brando in the Book of
Deuteronomy."

Lucille's red shoes clunked, one after the other, to the floor.
"But there is one somewhere," she replied. She saw her reflection
in the window. "Some brides we are, Lily." Lucille touched the lace
at her neck.

"Why do you want to go to the river, Nana?"

She could easily have gotten away, it was just white package
twine from the drawer in the kitchen where they kept scotch tape
and scissors and rubber jar rings....

A Population of Birds

Rose pushed the bedroom door shut. She stood with a cautious hand on the knob, her head bent, and waited. No whimpers, no imploring voices, no crockery shattering on the kitchen floor? Not even a ringing telephone? The bolt clicked in the latch, and she released the knob, but remained at the door, prepared to jump out into the hallway again and pretend she had never stepped inside the room at all.

The back door slammed, setting the duplex walls to trembling and dislodging one end of the curtain rod above the kitchen window. Putting the rod back in place was part of her daily tie-my-shoe-lace-kiss-it-better-spider-up-my-leg routine, but sometimes she stared at the loose end for several minutes before reaching for it. Those times it was almost too heavy to lift.

The house was a capsule of silence surrounded by the cries of children. There. She had a piece of the afternoon all to herself now.

With both hands, she pushed her hair away from her face and drifted towards her bathroom. Her bathroom! The irony of a "private bawth" in this cardboard house on a cardboard street that was all punched through by the fists of millions and millions of kids. But the sparkling glass tumbler beside the sink offered sanctuary in the gleam on its rim. She exhaled, then pulled a bottle from behind the waste-basket under the vanity. She poured two fingers of Scotch and kicked off her slippers. The latest copy of *Lady 21* lay open on her bedside table. A breeze from the window played with the corners of its pages. An American talk-show host smiled into the room, not caring that no one had smiled back at her all day. Rose had heard her name many times, but didn't know her. They couldn't get that channel on their TV. There was little money. The family lived cable-denied.

She was about to sit down on the bed when she heard a delicate scratching at the bedroom door. Clyde, the feline master of the house, wanted to share Rose's brief escape. He liked to lounge on the window sill and take the sun, and pretend that only birds populated the earth. Rose had seen the birds, too. Precious few tall trees in the neighbourhood, but there was one in front of her bedroom window. Sometimes birds fluttered among its leaves and branches. Clyde could only watch, being too old and stuffed with table-scraps to climb or pounce.

She admitted the cat, his greeting was whispered. He belonged here with her.

Rose lit a cigarette. The Scotch evaporated on her tongue, she took such tiny sips to make it last. Curled up among the pillows on her single cot, she wiggled her toes and picked up the magazine. Marriage, separation, divorce, remarriage, child-rearing, success stories, romantic interiors, silky exteriors — all flipped by under Rose's damp thumb. What should she read today? Not a decision to make in a hurry. Divorce was out of the question. Her own had been most unbeguiling, nothing like the ones in the glossies. The redhead two bays over had fewer children, more channels on her TV, a silky exterior, and she actually liked football. "Rose," she remembered her husband saying that very first of dark days, "I met a broad at the 7-11 just now who actually likes football! We each bought a newspaper and — it was so funny, Rose — we both looked at the sports page before we left the store! We had a good laugh about it." Ha. Ha. What a long time ago that seemed, a long arduous unravelling of neatly-woven expectations.

At last, a pair of dark brown eyes invited her with the same gleam as the Scotch glass. He was a classical pianist, she read. Good. She had played the piano when she was a girl. Her pudgy fingers had arched and pranced on the yellowed keys of her father's piano, and he had hummed and conducted from his usual chair. It was still her favourite instrument. She could recognize Chopin and Rachmaninoff when the pitiful old radio, from its lair in a corner of the kitchen counter, would permit it. Hearing the piano mornings when she was alone, Rose would drop her dishrag in the breakfast rubble and grab the tinny portable to turn it this way and that until the melodies were pure, the static vanquished. Then she would sag onto a chair and loosen her nerves and muscles, until one child or another, often not even her own, would explode into the room. Where did they come from, those mornings? They were always just there. Perhaps they hid in the broom closet or underneath the fridge, waiting for her to soften.

The tinkling of sonatinas wove in and out among the words on the page, and Rose became the pianist portrayed by the words and his lover at the same time. In the brown eyes of the man in the glossy photos, she caught images of her father, who had died young, dreaming away their poverty with the piano and the company of his children.

The back door banged, the wall quaked. In a remote corner of her mother-brain, she registered the weight and pace of the footsteps in the kitchen below. It was only Eric. He hardly even acknowledged her, ever. At seventeen, he was his own man, with a girlfriend and a cashier job at the car wash.

The Scotch slid from the clear brittle glass, the sleek pages of the magazine turned and turned, the cigarette glowed, the black cat dozed on the sill, softened like molasses in the sun. The tranquility absorbed her. There was always a certain climax to the escape ritual, a moment when she neither remembered the morning's crises, nor anticipated the inevitable interruption and end of the escape, usually a cry of "Ma!" from one of the younger children. Always a moment of total fantasy and peace which was not sleep.

The footsteps padded on the worn hallway rug up to her door, then stopped. Rose's foot jerked and her eyes shifted to the door.

That was wrong. His footsteps never stopped there. Come on. Four more, to the next door.

"Ma?" The word hung in the air like a feather. Rose put the glass on the table, the cigarette in a saucer, and was about to reply, "Yes?" when the latch clicked, the knob turned, and the door opened. Rose admired the calmness and deliberation with which the door moved in its quarter-circle path. The younger children always threw it open, as if their day were a never-ending game of hide-and-seek.

Eric stood there, one hand on the door-frame, the other limp at his side, as though the door had opened on its own. His gaze was already fixed on her. Had he been able to see her through the wood?

Rose stared at her eldest child, and in a milli-second recorded his sallow complexion, sickly-dark eyes, his thinness. Why hadn't she seen those things before? She had noted the chubbiness of her youngest child, the murky beauty of her middle daughter, the grace of her athletic twelve-year-old.

Something about Eric in the doorway made Rose sad. Something about that hand hanging at his left side, its fingers loose. It was an innocent hand, yet a man's hand. How could that be? It was also the hand of her father. Her eyes focussed on Eric's again, where they lingered as he came into the room.

Rose sat up on the edge of the bed. The cat stretched and yawned and jumped to the floor, and brushed against Eric's legs. Eric lifted him to his shoulder, and said nothing. Clyde leaned against the side of his head and purred. Rose reached up to touch Eric's shirt where it buttoned along his meagre chest. When had the little boy left his body? When would her other babies vanish, leaving strangers behind? What if she didn't notice the switch? Would she always find out too late? All that remained of the child Eric was the partially opened fly on his faded corduroy jeans. The tab stuck out just the way it did on little Janie's trousers. Was that something other mothers could mend?

The cat clunked to the floor and Eric moved towards the window. Rose sat still and tried to imagine what he wanted. Should she speak, natter in a mother-like way, or wait for him to make a beginning? His call to her from the other side of the door was still suspended between them. She would wait, let the man introduce himself to his mother.

He picked up the magazine. It fell open at the picture of the pianist. Eric sat down beside Rose and scanned the page.

"This guy's dead," he announced. His voice was flat. Rose frowned. What did he mean? Musically? "His wife's lover shot him. It was on the radio last week." He glanced at his mother. Usually, he avoided any conversation about broken marriages or adultery. When the topic came up, as it did time and time again, he would give Rose that sharp look to see how she was reacting.

"No one's safe," she answered as she gazed once more into the paper eyes of the minutes-old, now-dead idol. She stood up and carried the saucer of ashes to the bathroom and scraped them with a square of tissue into the toilet. When she went back to the bedroom Eric was curled up on the pillows where she had been just moments earlier. He was smoking. She had never seen him smoke before and had always believed that he did not. This is my cue, she thought, to lecture my teen-aged son on the evils of tobacco. She placed the saucer with a firm clack on the table beside him.

She sat again at the foot of the bed and considered the problem of the Scotch. Should she drink it in front of him? Spill it in the sink? Ignore it? Offer him a sip? A glass? He was leafing through the magazine, but when Rose looked at him now, she saw that his eyes were not taking anything in. He glanced at the Scotch and she thought he would reach for it and take a drink. Instead, he stuck his hand into his jacket pocket and took out the little packages of mustard and ketchup and butter and jam that he collected at hamburger joints and coffee shops. Rose always dumped them into the egg bin in the refrigerator and used them when they ran out of their own supply. That happened often. Eric emptied both pockets and piled them all beside the tumbler.

"Bringing home the bacon?"

"Too greasy," he mumbled. "Leaves a stain in my jacket." He flipped through the magazine, nonchalant.

She kept her voice casual. "Have you seen Dad this week?"

Eric butted the cigarette, suddenly, as though she'd commanded him to. "Yeah. Yesterday. He came down here." Rose's face
clouded. "You weren't around," he continued. "He wants me to go
to a game with him tomorrow night."

"Great," said Rose. "Just the two of you?"

"I don't know." He was hedging. "I'm not sure. I think he said
Helen might go if they can get a sitter and everything." He flipped
the magazine faster, faster.

Rose picked imaginary lint from her brown sweater. So?

Eric erupted. "Why do you wear that crummy old rag?" His
expression turned sullen.

Rose stared at her son in surprise. "What do you mean? It's a
comfortable old sweater. I wouldn't throw it away." He should
talk—he wears that denim jacket twenty-four hours a day.

"It's summer, Ma. Haven't you noticed? Look. That tree out
there has green leaves. That means it's summer, Ma."

The tree has birds, thought Rose. This is my room and seasons
don't count up here, she wanted to say, but bit her tongue. He was
right. Helen never looked shabby. "Your old mother is becoming
susceptible to drafts, Sonny." She forced a thin smile.

Eric tossed the magazine onto the table and examined a chronic
hang-nail on his thumb.

Now.

"They want me to move in with them over there. To live.
They've asked me a couple of times already."

Rose knew. Harry and Helen were apparently a fun couple.
They hoped to rescue poor Eric from his dreary life with three little
brats and a threadbare excuse for a mother.

"And what do you say when they ask you?" Rose asked. Lord,
what do I expect him to answer, 'I say thank you, Mommy'?

"I just say I'll see, and I'll talk to you about it. So now I am." He
wriggled out of his place in the corner among the pillows, stood,
and leaned with both hands on the table. Near the window Clyde
washed a mutilated ear with a blunt paw. Eric looked at the glass of
Scotch for a moment, then out beyond the window pane. His next
question was not impatient, as it might have been. "So what do you

think?"

Rose remained seated on the bed, her hands tucked safely between clenched thighs. "I think... I think the children will miss you. I think you won't find things as rosy over there as you imagine." If he asked about that one, she would not explain. "I think Dad would like to have his only son around for a couple of years before you move out on your own, and perhaps that makes the most sense." She could say much more, but where to fix the amount of long-harboured emotion she could set free at this point?

Then he was talking again, about the view from her window. "You can't see much of the street from here, can you? That tree hides a lot of it."

"I never thought about it. I expect your landscape doesn't look much different from mine. The tree is in front of your window, too, after all." Rose stood at Eric's side, and they both gazed into the tree where some finches darted about, searching for seeds, unwary of the menacing cat.

"It is different, though, Ma. I don't see as much of the tree when I look out as I do the street. I can see almost everything that happens out there." Eric put his hands on the window frame. The suddenness with which he raised the window startled Rose and frightened the birds. They flew away. "The other day I was watching the Foleys move out of the house across the street. They had somebody's half-ton down there, and Mrs. Foley was bitching at Mr. Foley because he was drunk again and he was dropping stuff and there was crap all over their driveway. He spilled a sack of potatoes. There were potatoes rolling onto the street. Didn't you hear them yelling? You were up here, too."

Rose felt his eyes and she shook her head.

"And then all of a sudden I see this one potato that isn't a potato. It's orange and it's rolling into the street from our yard. And then I realize that the kids are playing with Janie's sponge ball in front of the house, here just underneath our rooms. Didn't you hear them?"

Again Rose shook her head. No, she hadn't heard anything or seen anything. A curious irritation tingled at the back of her mind.

"They're not supposed to play in the front. They know that." But how can I stop them?

"They were playing there that day, Ma. Geez, I've chased them off the lawn hundreds of times, you know that. Haven't you ever heard me yelling from my window?"

"Yes, I've heard you, and you know I remind Janie and her friends almost every day to stay in the back with the gate shut." She groped for the cigarettes. She wanted him to leave so she could listen to the music. "I don't like it that you smoke."

"This is only the second time I've had a cigarette and I don't like it, either. It just seemed to be the thing to do in this room."

"Dad and Helen smoke all over the place."

"I know." He put his finger through a hole in the window screen. "Geez, this place could use some fixing up."

He was so tall. Like her father and his father, her husband. Hands with long fingers, belligerence beneath empathy. She felt lost in triangles of want and possession and loss, the desire to touch, to keep away, to mother. She looked at the plastic envelopes of ketchup and mustard on the night table and blinked away sudden tears.

At last a bird appeared in the tree. "I don't know about that Helen. She looks at me funny sometimes," said Eric. "I get the feeling she wants to grab me. She wears this neon lipstick."

Thank goodness he'll let me laugh instead. Rose answered, "Well, at least you can see her coming." More finches returned to the tree. "Let's think about it, let's think about it. Not about Helen's leers, about...."

"Maybe I should finish my story," Eric went on. "I see this sponge ball bouncing among the potatoes, and then what do I see? I see Janie go bouncing after it, out into the street, and there's this car coming around the curve, too fast, as usual." He could talk — they had no car. "And it almost hit her, Ma. He had to swerve so's not to hit her. Man, I almost had a heart attack."

"No one mentioned this to me!" Rose cried. "No one told me!"

"I went down right away and they were all standing around on the porch. Janie was crying. They asked me not to tell you, so I chased them all into the back yard and had a long talk with them. I described a cat I once saw hit by a car. Scared 'em half to death."

Rose hugged Eric's arm. "Poor Janie," she whispered. He clutched at her arm but only pinched the material of her sweater.

Bang. The back door again. Little feet running through the kitchen and up the stairs, almost to Rose's door before she could react. The wailing "Maa! Maa!" began at the top of the stairs. Rose and Eric both stepped back, away from each other. The door flew open.

Rose caught her breath at the spectre of Janie, bent forward and panting in the doorway. Her arms stood away from her body as though she were about to leap across the threshold. Behind her, three friends gawked in the door. Blood trickled across her lips and down her chin.

"Look, Ma! My first nosebleed!"

"Not mine." Rose used the hem of her sweater to wipe the corners of Janie's mouth. "We'll clean it up downstairs, Hon'."

The staircase was a tunnel of rustling nylon as Janie and her crew went down to the kitchen. "You could begin some fixing up by making it so that the curtain rod doesn't fall when the back door slams," Rose flung over her shoulder to Eric. If we can only keep that curtain rod from falling down.

"It would be easier to stop the door slamming."

"You have a lot to learn, my boy," said Rose, slipping the sweater off her arms. "A door will bang in a house like this as long as it stands. And sponge balls will roll among potatoes." She picked up the magazine and opened it to the picture of the dead pianist. "Do you think I should hang it up on my closet door, like James Dean?"

"Maa!"

Rose put on her slippers, but as she left her room, she paused in the doorway to look at Eric. He was scratching Clyde's thick neck with his innocent, manly hand. All the birds had returned to the tree now, and he watched their movements among the leaves. A sonatina played in Rose's head and she hummed louder and louder as she marched downstairs to heal the wounded.

Fish Pedlar

Moist August night air seeped through the window screens of the square farm house, dampening the saltines so that they would crumble at next day's dinner, and souring the soiled shirts in the laundry basket. Tussock moths boomed against the barrier screens. In an upstairs bedroom Terry folded a flannel nightgown by lamplight. She went to the window and listened to the brittle chirping of night crickets. The half moon was yellowed by the smoke of forest fires, smoke transported by a northern breeze that also carried cool dewy air. A southerly wind would clear away the smoke and dry up the grain for harvest.

The woman thought, finally, about the garden. Dressed only in a man's shirt, she went barefoot down the walk, across the lawn, and along the dirt path to the strip of tilled earth beside the young poplar hedge. The shadows there, the very ones that had frightened her when she was a child, now remained only shadows, and she passed through their emptiness on purpose instead of keeping to the mercury-lit path.

Already August, and this was the first time she had been to the vegetable garden. Brick had planted it one afternoon at the end of May, later than most people. He'd held off as long as he could, waiting for her to announce that she was ready for it, ready to go out with him and drop seeds into his arrow-straight furrows, and impale empty packets onto the stakes at the end of each row so that they wouldn't mistake parsley for carrots when the green came through.

But she didn't announce. One Sunday he'd scrambled through the collection of old seeds stored in the back porch, and made his garden. She had stayed in the house, and neither had spoken for the rest of the day.

In the following weeks, he brought radishes to the kitchen table and offered them to her like rubies. She would find fresh young lettuce leaves tucked into the refrigerator crisper among the heads she'd bought at the supermarket. And everyone, everyone, asked, "How's your garden?" That's all they asked. At first she lied, mouthing conventional gardener's phrases. But at last, she'd begun to reply, "I don't know. I haven't been in it."

Now there was dew on the plants. The cold leaves brushed against her legs. The collie, catching her scent in the damp air, came down the path and wagged his tail when his nose touched Terry's foot.

The trunk of an old willow leaned in silhouette against the glow of the town lights and lingering redness from a vanished sun. As Terry gazed in its direction, her eyes detected two movements: an owl on the branch raised its wings and soared downward until it was skimming just above the surface of the ground, and a car that had been chasing its light beams along the road appeared straight-on at the head of the driveway. Terry was caught for a moment between the flight of the owl, and the urgency of the car's approach. Then, remembering her naked legs, she backed into the shadows. The collie was barking now. It wasn't Brick coming home from the field. Terry stumbled from shadow to shadow until she was safe in the darkness behind the house. The car's motor died at the garage. One door slammed.

The barking became more furious, but underneath it, Terry could hear a man's voice, low and even, unafraid; then, firm knocks at the front door. She froze against the cool wooden siding of the house while the visitor waited on the veranda. But when the footsteps retreated back along the sidewalk, Terry slipped through the back door and pulled on her gardening jeans, torn and streaked with old dirt. Then she ran through the house, out the front door, and along the sidewalk towards the unfamiliar car. Strangers calling on farms seldom rushed away when they found no one there. They tended to pause, to try to get a feeling for the place, and there was always the chance that someone might be in the granary or the garden.

"Arthur Klady." His hand was stretched towards her, palm up, fingers curled. Terry placed her hand in his and saw his teeth glittering beneath the shade of his hat brim.

"Terry. And Tib." She gestured towards the growls without taking her eyes from the man's face. He dropped to his knees and spoke softly to the dog, saying its name over and over. Terry fumbled for her next words. "I'm sorry—I wasn't—I didn't—" Klady tilted his hat back and looked up at her. "My husband isn't home. Is it him you wanted to see?"

"Well, that depends. If you like, I'll tell you my business, and then I'll leave and come back another time. When your husband is home. If you prefer." He turned and went to his car. He limped a little, as though one foot were asleep. A torn pocket dangled from the seat of his pants. He reached through the open window and brought out a leather-covered folder. "I'm a pedlar, I'll warn you," he said.

She hadn't seen a door-to-door salesman since she'd moved to the farm from the town. But she remembered the shabby, grizzled old men who appeared from time to time at her parents' farm home, men wearing smelly clothes and driving dilapidated pick-up trucks loaded with blocks of ice. "You used to sell fish."

"Fish?"

"I'm sorry. Forget it."

He handed her the folder and remained silent while she opened it. The picture inside startled her. It was a face, but not a real one, one moulded from some kind of metal. It was dark, swarthy-looking, but its hard, smooth features reminded Terry of a human skull. She thought at first the face was a man's, but when she turned it more to the light from the mercury lamp, she saw by the lips and the hair that it was a woman's. There were other pictures, the faces all different, some in profile, one of a bearded man. Expressionless faces with smooth, empty eyes, all carved in greatest detail, but unfamiliar to her.

Klady looked at the house. "You have a fine oak door on your home. And no doorbell. One of these might look handsome up there, and it would be functional." He grinned with relief. "There. That's my spiel."

"A door-knocker? That's what these are? Door-knockers?"

"Sculpted in your image."

"A far cry from fish."

A nighthawk on the wing preceded their slow return to the house. The bird's erratic flight was like one of Brick's electronic airplanes, the way it changed direction and altitude at the whim of a hand on the transmitter.

The kitchen was cleaned up and lit by a bulb above the sinks. Only Brick's peanut butter knife lay on the counter where he'd taken a dollop for dessert after supper. Terry watched Klady to see how he would approach the room. As though knowing her thoughts, he glanced about the kitchen before looking at her face again. Red brick wallpaper on two walls, light oak cabinets on the others, gauzy curtains striped vertically in earth colours, a spindly vine hanging at the window. Lead glass light fixture, tomato sauce on the carpet. She gave him a few seconds to make a comment, but he said nothing.

"Coffee? Tea?"

"You a tea-drinker?"

"Not alone," she laughed. "But Brick — my husband — is a connoisseur. And I'll have some if you will."

"Good." Klady sat down in her chair at the table. He leaned forward with his arms stiff and his hands resting on his knees. As Terry prepared the pot, out of the corner of her eye she saw him remember his hat and place it on the radiator next to the table. He began to speak, but she cut in. "Do you always do your work so late at night?" She tried to make her eyes twinkle.

"Well, I was around earlier in the day, and lots of people weren't home." He threw up his hands, palms up. "Most places, coming back didn't help."

Terry sat in Brick's chair, which forced her to look at Klady's outline against the light. It was a new perspective and she was surprised to see the fine bristles on his chin and the prominent bridge of his nose. He could see her face lit up, she knew, and she stood to check the kettle.

His voice was changed. "Maybe I should just come back another time," he said. "You'd probably rather I didn't sit around here all evening." He didn't say "waiting" and he didn't get up from the chair. His shoulders had sunk a little.

"No, it's fine. Refreshing for me. Not many people drop in here, just old friends." She emphasized the *old*. "Besides, most places coming back doesn't help." They laughed together. He adjusted his chair and she heard him stretching out his legs in front of him. She imagined him scratching the top of his head, the way her father had done when he came in from a long day's work, and expected, when she turned around, to see his hair tousled. But he was looking at her. "Almost done," she said. She sat down. "Do you smoke?"

"Not alone." They laughed again. He took a package from his jacket pocket. But, instead of holding it towards her, he took out a cigarette and handed it to her. She was moved by the touched cigarette, and kept her eyes lowered as he lit it and his own with a wooden match.

After a moment, she asked, "So what do you need? A photograph?"

"No, not a photograph. Photographs falsify the subject. You know, shadows, light, angles, background, dirty lenses." He leaned forward a little and peered into her face. The gesture was unintrusive. "No, I need your structure." He pulled a yellow pencil from the breast pocket of his shirt and rolled it between his fingers.

Terry took her eyes from his and focussed on the pencil. "Looks painless."

Klady did not reply immediately. His eyebrows rose slightly, and then his eyes narrowed and he pursed his lips. He touched her cheek with the point of the pencil. "That depends," he said. The pencil slipped along the fine-boned line of her jaw. "People are never quite the same after they've put themselves at the mercy of a conjuror. Or a salesman." He sketched her forehead in the air, and her eyes, and the unshadowed side of her nose. Terry was afraid to move for a moment, though her eyes followed the pencil.

The kettle blew before he got to her mouth. Terry hurried to the stove and lifted the kettle from the heat, watching Klady in its bright chrome surface. She saw him put the pencil behind his ear. They spoke at the same time.

"Milk and sugar?"

"I drink mine straight."

"Right," said Terry. "Straight."

While waiting for the brew, she gathered lemon, mint, spoons, and, after some hesitation, Cointreau onto a wicker tray. The tray wasn't necessary. She could have placed everything on the table in front of him, one by one, but it would have been — kitchenish. She used the china cups.

"So," he began as he added Cointreau to the greenish-black tea in his cup. "What do you do?"

He was the first. And not a mention of the garden so far. She laughed out loud.

"Are you a farmer's wife? A farmer? None of the above?"

She shook her head. "I'm afraid not. I'm afraid not."

He was relaxed and easy now. "Afraid?"

"Well, I mean — one is expected to be. A farmer's wife, I mean. I do other things."

"I thought so."

"I don't really have to say what they are, do I? Now that you know I do them." They looked at each other over the rims of their flowered china cups.

"Would it be heavy?" she asked. "Could I take it with me if — I wanted to?" His complacency was disquieting. "Or would it be cumbersome?"

"It might be. It's not a large object though. Not much heavier than—that cookbook, say."

She followed his gaze. "It's a dictionary."

"Ah. See? I still make mistakes."

She persisted. "How does it attach to the door? What part of my head would hit the plate? My chin?"

He straightened up and scanned the perimeter of her face.

"No," he murmured. "I think—your shoulder. You see, I would have your head tilted towards your shoulder, like this." He pushed against her cheek-bone with the back of his hand.

"So it would be this shoulder?"

"I think not. I think the other."

A feeble cry sounded in the outdoor air and, faint though it was, snagged the attention of both of them. Klady rose and took his cup to the door window. Terry looked into the light and smoothed back her hair. The gentle squawking came again. This time she could see his image in the window above the sink.

"There's two of them out there, flying like mad."

"Two, now...."

"Man, they can really go. They're acrobats, almost." Klady remained at the door, speaking into the dimly lit yard.

Terry addressed the reflection. "Can't walk or even stand worth a damn, though. Weak feet. They just sort of recline all day long. I accidentally scared one up in the daytime once. Or rather, Tibni did. It was roosting on a brush-pile out back. It flew all around just the way they're doing now, only it looked so strange in the daylight, when you're used to seeing it at night." She bent forward slightly. "I felt sorry for it. Guilty."

She was startled by Klady's boisterous laughter. "Disturbing the spirits of the gods, eh?" He came back to his chair and refilled his cup.

"Does your wife have one hanging on your front door at home?"

His lips smiled. "She took hers with her." Then his eyes.

Terry felt as though she had been congealed in her chair for an eternity, and her arm jerked forward on the table so that the liquid in his cup rippled and splashed over the brim into the saucer.

Klady leaned back in the chair and stretched his arms above his head, more as if he were trying to touch something above him than to loosen tight muscles. The pencil caught in his sleeve and slipped to the floor. His eyes were closed now and his expression blank. With hands resting on either side of his neck, he spoke through his veiled eyes. "Home was hard to be at afterwards. I couldn't be still. It started even before she left. Marianne. I felt, somehow, vulnerable sitting in one spot for even an hour, much as I thought I wanted it while I was working. She took nothing of mine when she left. So I decided to use up my nest-egg and travel, and practise a useful hobby at the same time. I'd been taking snapshots of brides a lot of years. The embarrassment over unpretty fingernails and too much gum showing became tedious. I could hide the unprettiness, set up the lies, day after day. I just couldn't settle into an easy chair with those cover-ups in the evenings when it was all over."

Terry picked up the pencil. "Your wand."

Leaning forward, he grabbed it, held it point up, between them, and looked into her eyes. "I'll start with this, and I'll add another dimension, and then — you'll see. Or you won't. And either will be truth-telling." The pencil turned between his fingers. He shifted his thumb and for a moment Terry thought he would snap it in two, but he put it into his shirt pocket.

The starting up of the refrigerator and renewed squawking of the nighthawks outside began together.

Terry said, "You must spend some time at home."

"Oh, I go to the house to do the sculpting and the casting, whenever I've got a few orders together and the sketches are done, but.... And it isn't the loneliness that gets to me. It isn't that." Klady grabbed for the cigarettes. "See — when I'm finished a face I can hardly wait to take it to its owner and show it, to hold it out and say, 'This is you. Look. Feel.' And I leave them together, imagining what might happen between them. Is that *home?*" He looked at Terry with fresh intensity. "Can something like that be *home?*"

She stared through the thin cloud of smoke mulling above the ashtray, stared even through and beyond the walls.

Then Klady was on his feet with his hat in his hand, standing at the open wooden door. His fingers touched and probed the smoothness of the oak as if searching for hieroglyphics carved into its surface.

"Will you be back soon?" Terry felt her body rise from the chair.

"No."

"Fish pedlars are rare."

"Shall I do the sketch?"

She touched the door where he had, stroking across the grain. "Yes."

"I'll come back tomorrow. You haven't asked the price."

They walked out onto the veranda. From where they stood, they could both see two brilliant lights burning at last at the head of the driveway. Klady made a fastidious task of putting on his hat and adjusting the brim.

Terry did not look at him. "Tomorrow?" She watched the two headlights coming nearer and nearer on the drive. Brick never hurried down the driveway at the end of his day the way he did when he was just stopping by for a meal or a tractor part. He always drifted home after dark. If Terry was out in the yard, and it was a calm night, she could hear him coming when he was still miles away. "Not tomorrow. But—come back."

Klady was a shadow moving under the elm tree spreading over the walk. In an instant, he was in his car with the engine running. They would pass each other on the driveway. It was right that they had not met, had not seen each other, had not touched each other's hand.

Hunting Clouds

The Cat was finally dead. She looked small, dead. The rock Luther had chosen was flecked with obsidian and pocked with fool's gold. It was larger than the Cat and prettier. The two were tied together with fish line.

When Luther and I pushed the canoe into the lake, pebbles ground at its hull at one end and sand hissed at the other. I paddled at the front, Luther sat in the stern to practise his steering. Between us lay the Cat and the rock. It was almost midnight.

"The moon is gorgeous," said Luther.

He had just learned that word, gorgeous, yesterday. Mellowed with brandy, I had told him he was gorgeous.

"What means gorgeous?" he'd asked. Luther had sort of a breathless way of talking and permanently messy dark hair and a smile that knocked your socks off.

"It means Paul McCartney. And Jane Fonda."

"What means beautiful?"

"Loons in the morning."

And then this morning, while standing in front of the cottage, listening for the loon, Luther found the Cat. Dead and under the veranda. I was annoyed that an exchange student from Germany should have to find a dead cat under his host's veranda, but even more, I felt bad about the Cat. It had been difficult enough to come back here.

She'd been lurking around Bruno's for years. She didn't belong to him, though, but roamed the lakefront from cottage to cottage, birthing kittens, resisting affection, hunting mice, eating barbecued steak bones and corn-on-the-cob and ends of wieners. She always turned up at wiener roasts. First, you'd see her spotty yellow eyes glowing in the poison ivy patch, then her whole body slinking nearer as the wiener ends began to plop in the grass. I'd known the Cat for as long as I'd been coming to Bruno's cottage at the lake, but Natalie had been the only one who could get near her.

"Let us make a burial at sea," Luther had suggested. "She belongs to the lake, yes?"

We laid her out beside the fire-pit and had a wiener-roast wake, Bruno and Karen and Luther and I. I could not eat, hadn't all day. Everything had been fine yesterday, comfortable and familiar. But this morning, Natalie's not being here and finding the Cat dead had twisted my stomach into a knot.

And then Luther tied the Cat to the rock he'd picked up beside the dock. "We would not like her to float back to the shore," he said.

We paddled far out into the lake, then drifted for a while and watched the moon on the water. Other fires flickered in front of cottages along the shore. We could hear Billie Holiday singing "Gone With The Wind" out of Bruno's cassette player, and somewhere else Mick Jagger was belting out "Ruby Tuesday."

"This is what I will remember about Canada," said a voice behind me. "The gorgeous moon, loons in the morning, and sunsets. And making a canoe ride at midnight." I imagined it was the Cat talking. "There, it is on twelve."

"I don't want to look." I still wasn't sure I wanted the burial at sea. I pictured the bloated body of the Cat covered with leeches, bound to the glittering rock. Luther had said, "But what happens to it under the earth?"

He let the Cat and the rock slip into the water. They hardly made a sound.

A light breeze came up. We were drifting to shore, so we paddled back towards the middle of the lake and rested again. The full moon had climbed strong and high above us, the sky was bright. Small pieces of cloud raced past the moon. "Ah, now we say in German, *Die Wolken jagen* — the clouds are hunting." We watched them in silence for a moment. "*Die Wolken jagen*. Like something moving very quickly alone, hunting, but there is nothing that can be seen to hunt. Like — like a Porsche driving very fast at night on an empty highway."

He was right. The clouds looked like wolves migrating across a frozen northern lake — grey with silver edges, lean and hungry. "I lost my sister here," I said.

"Bruno and Karen told me about your sister. She has died?"

"Yes. Last summer, just after we left here."

"But you said, you lost her here."

"I did. Not her body, though."

"This is a puzzle."

"Two years ago, two summers ago, her husband went out fishing, with a man from one of the cottages. Bruno stayed back to finish reshingling the roof, and Natalie and I don't — didn't care for fishing. He never came back, they didn't. We waited until it was well past dark. Natalie kept running across the lawn to the dock to look for their boat. We went to the store and called the R.C.'s, of course, and they went out on a search. It was a night very like this, clear and full of moon."

I was talking with my back still turned to Luther. I thought of twisting around and facing him, but it was so calm, and I didn't want him to see my face.

"Finally Natalie just stayed on the dock. She sent me away. It was cold that night, and I brought her a blanket. I remember how she just sat there, huddled under that white blanket in the moonlight. I'd go out to her, to try to get her in the cottage, but she was frozen to that dock. She didn't say anything, just wouldn't let me touch her.

"At sunrise, the R.C.'s came to the cabin, and before they could say the words, we and Natalie saw their patrol boat pulling Bruno's motorboat across the lake. It was empty. That's the way they'd found it, beyond the tunnels that go through the rock at the far end of the lake.

"Natalie believed they'd gone hunting in the woods for something, something had lured them out of the boat, and they got lost. There was a big search, but....

"When Natalie saw the patrol boat towing that empty boat across the lake, she watched it till she couldn't see it any more, and then turned towards the cabin, and for a moment, I thought she was coming in. She saw the R.C.'s in the veranda. And she went to the rocks beside the dock and picked up a great big one, and held it high over her head and threw it with all her might into the lake, like she was trying to kill the lake.

"And that's when I lost her. She snapped, at that moment, I think. After that, we could lead her around like a lamb. We took her back to the city while the search went on, but she was never the same.

"The next year was very bad. We thought she just needed time, time, time. But she slipped away, further and further. I think — if only she'd seen him die, or seen his body, it would have been different. But the waiting and not knowing drove her insane.

"The weirdest thing was the Cat. Natalie could touch her, even make her purr. There was something about Natalie that pacified animals. But last year, just before she died, I brought her here, hoping to jolt her old spirit. She couldn't have gotten any worse. The Cat came out of the bushes, attracted, I think, by the sound of her voice, though she spoke little. But the Cat wouldn't go near her. I coaxed and manipulated Natalie into the position she'd always used to call the Cat to her, bent over, one hand out in front of her, the other on her knee, but the Cat knew. For the rest of the week we'd see her, stealing about the cottage, smelling Natalie's smell, hearing her say the odd word, but unable to find her."

Something bumped against the bottom of the canoe. I looked into the water. "Is it a log?" asked Luther.

"I don't know," I said. It was the Cat, I thought, come back to life and free of the rock, like Houdini.

"Where is it? Can you see it?"

"No."

It bumped the canoe again, this time on the side, near Luther. We kept still and scanned the water, looking for some sign of a log, or a body.

"Probably a ski," I muttered. I looked to the shore. Everything around us had changed while we were staring into the lake. "Look what's happening!" I cried.

The cottage lights and the fires were only pin-points on the shore, yellowish and dim. The trees and outlines of buildings had vanished.

"It is a fog," said Luther.

"More likely the breeze is carrying smoke from the forest fires up north."

Another thud, louder. "There!" Luther whispered. "Paddle to the right a bit."

"Is it a ski?"

"No," he said. He crawled to the centre of the canoe and put his hand over the side. "It feels to me like a *Kahlkopf.*"

"What?"

He laughed. "A bald head. I cannot grasp it, it keeps escaping." I heard his fingers scrabbling in the water. "I think it is a watermelon," he said.

"A watermelon?"

"Yes, I'm sure. Move to your left and lean a little. Not too much. I will try to stab it with a knife." He opened his pocketknife and crouched over the side while I tried to hold the canoe steady. Over my shoulder I could see him make a short, sharp thrust downward. Our canoe rocked and the water gurgled beneath us. Then, with his other hand, he cupped the melon and heaved it into the boat.

"Who would have thought a watermelon could float?" I said. "I would expect it to sink like a stone."

"It is strange, yes? To find a watermelon floating in the lake at midnight, with a full moon in the sky and a smoke-fog around us? Even more strange that it comes to our canoe?"

I knew exactly where the watermelon had come from. The

Peckhams next door had taken their weekend guests out on their houseboat for the day. I'd seen them motor by this afternoon while I was on the dock, and they'd been eating watermelon and tossing rinds into the lake. They were a little drunk, and I wasn't surprised that during their carousing a watermelon should have been thrown overboard. It had probably gone in on the opposite side of the lake. All evening it had been making its way back to the Peckhams, drifting with the current. I did not tell Luther this.

"Do you think it is safe to eat?" he asked. I could hear his knife slash into the melon and the juicy splitting of the flesh.

"Yes, I'm sure it is. I'm hungry."

"Turn around."

He'd cut the fruit in half. The melon was small, probably home-grown. With his Swiss Army knife, Luther carved out crisp wedges and handed them to me on the blade. "How did she die?"

"Drugs. Accidental, I think. Though I often wonder if she knew the Cat couldn't recognize her and took it as a sign."

"It is not usual to lose your mind when your husband dies."

"No. It was just something about Natalie. But — it's made me afraid. Afraid that a loss of someone I love will make me insane, like her. We were sisters. How much like her am I?"

"But you already have the answer. You are not like her. The Cat never went to you, did it? And you have lost someone you loved — Natalie. And here you are, still sane, yes?"

"I don't know. I suppose I am. Insane things happen around me. Like finding this watermelon in the lake. Maybe this is what becomes of cats when they're buried at sea. Perhaps this is where I should have buried Natalie."

Billie was still crooning through the fog, though we couldn't quite make out the words. "Here's to the Cat," I said, raising my shard of watermelon.

"*Prost*," said Luther.

I wanted to stay there forever. But Luther eased up onto the strut and lifted his paddle. "The wind is more strong and coming from a different place. We should go back?"

"Yes."

"We will bring Bruno and Karen a gift. You do not need to paddle."

"I want to."

The smoke blew away while we skimmed towards the last lamp-post on the east side of the lake. As the air cleared, the glow of lights and fires radiated and trees regained their silhouettes. We could make out words now in the lilt of Billie Holiday's voice, words accompanied by a smouldering alto saxophone:

> *I can see the sun up high though we're caught in the*
> *   storm.*
> *I can see where you and I could be cozy and warm.*
> *Let the rain pitter-patter,*
> *For it really doesn't matter*
> *If the skies are grey.*
> *As long as I'm with you it's a lovely day.*

"Something more to remember when I go back to Germany," said Luther. "The gorgeous moon, loons in the morning, sunsets, and finding a watermelon in the lake in a smoke-fog."

I looked up. The clouds were still hunting past the cold, white moon. *"Die Wolken jagen,"* I said.

"Ja," said Luther.